a date
for
Hannah

High schooler Hannah has always been self-conscious about her weight, so when hottie swimmer Liam pays her extra attention at her sister's wedding, she has a hard time trusting his interest. Throughout the evening, Liam's charm wins her over until they're falling hard for each other. But the next day, Hannah learns something that may ruin it all.

a date for Hannah

New York Times Bestselling Author KATY REGNERY writing as

callie henry

For Henry and Callie.
You can finally read one.
I love you both more than words can ever say.

XOXOXO

Chapter One

Hannah

Hannah Giacomina didn't like dressing up.

In fact, any event that required a dress pretty much sucked.

It didn't matter that more and more clothing companies made dresses for bigger girls. She still felt like she was completely on display: her bigger-than-average chest strained against the neckline of her LC by Lauren Conrad junior plus-size dress, and the zipper in the back dug into her sensitive skin.

She chose to sit in the back row of chairs, scrunching down in her seat to be as inconspicuous as possible. The plastic rental chair creaked as her weight settled, and she froze for a second before relaxing. That's just what she needed: to break a folding chair and fall flat on her fat butt.

Once she was certain the chair wasn't going to embarrass her completely, she took a deep breath and sighed, looking at the program in her hand:

CEREMONY OF HOLY MATRIMONY
SABRINA GIACOMINA & TODD FILLMAN

Sabrina. Bree. Hannah's older sister.

Well, *half*-sister, to be specific—not that it mattered a bit to Hannah.

Glancing up from the program, she saw more and more guests arriving, taking their seats closer to the action. They were all about ten years older than Hannah, closer in age to Bree and Todd.

Hannah took a deep breath, feeling young and awkward all alone in the back row, but she quickly reminded herself that today wasn't about her: this was Bree's special day, and her sister had outdone herself in creating a fairy tale–worthy venue for her wedding. As an employee of I Tri Merli Cellars and Vineyard, she had been allowed to book the location for free, but the decorations were all Bree.

Light violin music floated on the breeze from the front of the orchard, where a quartet played classical pieces beside an archway covered in twinkle lights and white roses. At the end of each row of seating, there were big white bows tied to aisle chairs, and ivy trailed down in elegant bunches from the center of each bow to the floor. It was really beautiful, and Hannah felt a burst of pride as she thought of Bree's hard work to make everything perfect.

The purse on her lap buzzed, and Hannah withdrew her phone to find a text message from her mother.

MOM: Are you at the wedding? Everything okay?

Hannah rolled her eyes. It didn't matter that she was seventeen and had driven from their home in Brookings, Oregon, to visit Bree in Santa Rosa, California, at least a dozen times. Her mother still worried whenever she made the trip.

HANNAH: I'm fine, Mom. Everything's good. The wedding's about to start.

MOM: I love you, honey. Have fun!

Yeah, right, thought Hannah. *Have fun at a wedding where I don't know anyone and I'm probably the fattest and definitely the youngest guest. Sure thing. Great. Awesome. Thanks a lot, Mom.*

HANNAH: OK. ILY2. CU tomorrow.

"Hey, stranger!"

Hannah looked up, dropping the phone back into

her purse and grinning at her sister's best friend. "Abby!"

Bree was the head event planner at I Tri Merli Cellars and Vineyard, where Abby worked as a vintner and her husband, Scott, handled sales and marketing.

Abby's auburn hair caught the late afternoon sunlight and seemed even brighter and redder than usual. "Give me a hug, girl!"

Hannah jumped up and threw her arms around Abby, squeezing her tight.

"Hey! Why aren't you sitting the front?" Abby asked. "Bree saved you a seat."

"No, thanks," said Hannah, leaning away from her.

The seat that Bree had saved was in the family row, near Bree's mother, Giovanna. Giovanna *Giacomina*, who glared at Hannah every time she laid eyes on her.

Hannah understood why. When Bree was ten years old, their father, Lorenzo, had divorced Giovanna to marry Hannah's mother, Wendy, and Hannah was born six months later. The half-sisters had managed to form a bond with one another, but Giovanna wasn't able to forgive Wendy and Hannah for "stealing" Lorenzo. It made things very tense when Hannah and Giovanna were together.

"How are you and your mom doing?" asked Abby, her green eyes warm and kind.

Bree and Hannah's father had died of cancer four months ago, leaving Hannah's mother a widow and Lorenzo's two daughters grieving his loss.

"She has good days and bad days, but...we're okay."

"It'll take time," said Abby.

Hannah's eyes suddenly burned, and she blinked at her sister's friend, trying not to cry. It would ruin her makeup, and besides, it was bad enough to be sitting all alone. Sitting all alone and crying? Too pathetic for words.

"Hey, it's Hannah!" Scott's bright smile over Abby's shoulder saved the day. "You look gorgeous, young one."

Hannah shook her head like he was crazy but let him grab her for a hug just the same. She didn't like compliments and usually didn't accept them, but Abby's husband had always been kind to Hannah. It was impossible not to smile back at him.

"Thanks, Scott. Looking pretty sharp yourself."

Abby wore a Tiffany-blue, knee-length

bridesmaid dress, and Scott's tie was the same color blue with tiny white wedding dresses covering the shiny silk in a repeat pattern.

"Let me guess," said Hannah, grinning back and forth at the young couple, "Bree had those ties made specially?"

"You know Bree," said Abby with a soft chuckle.

Hannah *did* know Bree, and she loved her older sister to the moon and back. In fact, she couldn't think of anyone else on the face of the earth for whom she would not only *buy* but *wear* a dress.

Bree had always been special.

Even though their father had walked out on Bree when she was in fourth grade, her older sister had never held it against Hannah. In fact, Bree had been Hannah's idol since...well, *forever*. Ten years older, completely beautiful, and always ready with a hug and smile, Bree was amazing.

So amazing.

Sometimes maybe even...*too* amazing.

And that was the downside to being Bree's little sister: Bree was perfect. Perfect body, perfect hair, perfect clothes, perfect job, perfect wedding...and very soon, perfect husband.

While Hannah? Well, Hannah was *no one's* idea

of perfect. Baby fat had turned into teen fat and stuck around no matter how hard Hannah watched her calories or how often she visited the gym. When she and Bree stood side by side, Bree looked like a supermodel and Hannah felt like an elephant.

Depressed by the direction of her thoughts, Hannah looked around the orchard and pasted a fake smile on her face as she glanced back at Abby. "It looks really pretty here tonight—the flowers and bows and lights. Everything's beautiful."

"She outdid herself," said Abby. "She's just so awesome at everything she—"

"Hey, Abby?"

Hannah raised her gaze to the deep sound of a man's voice, and her jaw dropped.

Standing behind Scott and Abby was the handsomest boy Hannah had ever seen. At least six three, he stood a head taller than Scott and was wearing a white dress shirt with two open buttons at his throat. As Scott and Abby parted so that he could join them, Hannah's eyes slid to his arms. His shirt sleeves were rolled up, showcasing tan, muscular forearms dusted with a smattering of dark hair.

She stared at his arms for a second before raising her eyes to his face. Sky-blue eyes looked down at her, noticing her for the first time. His lips parted softly in surprise, and his glance flicked down to her chest before looking back up at her face. And then— for no reason at all—he smiled at her.

"Liam!" said Scott, slapping the younger man on the shoulder.

"H-Hey, Scott," said Liam, dragging his eyes away from Hannah. "Bree asked me to come find you. They're almost ready to get started."

Hannah's cheeks flushed when he returned his gaze to her. She hadn't looked away while he'd spoken to Scott. *Stop staring, Hannah. You're being super weird.*

But she couldn't. He was too handsome—plus, he was still smiling at her.

"I'm Liam," he said, stepping forward to offer her his hand. "And you are...?"

"This is Bree's little sister, Hannah," said Abby. "Hannah, Liam. Liam, Hannah. Liam's been giving us a hand in the vineyard this summer."

"Hi," whispered Hannah, her eyes locking with Liam's as she raised her hand to shake his.

His hand was like a mitt—huge, rough, and warm against hers—and though she generally considered herself a larger woman, she felt smaller than usual shaking his hand.

"Hey, Hannah," he murmured, his eyes tracing her features. He lingered for an extra second on her lips before meeting her gaze again, and it made her heart skip a beat as he shifted his palm against hers. "Good to meet you."

"You too," she answered, but as awesome as it was to touch him, it also made her uncomfortably aware of *her* body and *his* body and her immediate and blatant *attraction* to him.

She flushed, jerking her hand away.

"Time to go," said Abby. "See you kids later?"

Hannah's eyes darted back to her sister's friend. "Y-Yeah. Sure. Mm-hm. Yep."

Grinning like maybe she was hiding a chuckle, Abby pulled Scott away, disappearing into the crush of guests finding their seats for the ceremony.

"Are you here with anyone?" Liam asked, gesturing to the seat beside her.

"No," said Hannah, trying to compose herself. "Bree and I have the same father—um, *had* the same—but, um, different mothers, so I don't really know, um, anyone here. I mean, she's older than I am." Her cheeks were on fire with embarrassment. "Oh, my God. I'm babbling."

"Nah. It's fine." He lowered himself to the seat beside her in the otherwise empty row and shifted his body toward her. "Actually...I've already heard all about you."

"What do you mean?"

"Well...I *have* worked here all summer. I know you're Bree's half-sister and you're from Oregon." He glanced around. "I think you're the youngest guest here too."

He was right on all counts, but it was sort of disconcerting to have her private information handed to her. "Umm...stalker much?"

He grinned at her. "Touché."

"Anything you *don't* know?"

"Hmmm." His eyes scanned her face as he bit his lower lip. "I didn't know how pretty you were."

She chuckled in surprise, unaccustomed to flattery. Boys didn't flirt with the size-sixteen girl. They chose the fours and sixes for flirting and asked Hannah if they could borrow her science notes after class.

"Yeah, right."

"You think I'm kidding?" he asked. "Bree's totally hot, and I can totally see the resemblance between you two."

Like Hannah, Bree had their father's brown hair and brown eyes, but that was where the similarities ended. Bree was beautiful, petite, and graceful, while Hannah…well, *wasn't.*

She scoffed at him, looking away and sort of wishing he'd stop talking. "I think you might need glasses."

"And I think *you* might need a mirror."

Her lips parted in surprise and she blinked at him. "Seriously, how do you know so much about me?"

He shrugged. "My dad lives nearby. Like I said, I have a summer job here, and last week I heard Bree and Abby talking about Bree's younger sister who was coming down for the wedding. Between you and me? I was sorta glad there was going to be someone else here under thirty."

"Truth." She laughed, raising one eyebrow. "So you're *not* a stalker."

"Not *yet*," he said.

It was that *yet*—that beautiful, simple, one-syllable word—that made Hannah's smile wider and brighter.

Boys didn't *like* Hannah. Maybe they thought she was a nice person, but they didn't pay her any special attention. Not like this. Not like flirting and smiling and making her feel warm all over.

Was he for real? And was it terrible that she wanted him to be for real? That, for once, she wanted to be the girl with whom a cute boy chose to flirt?

Yeah, but you're not *that girl, Hannah-Hannah-Fat-as-Santa.*

That familiar, mocking voice whispered in her head, making all of her stupid hopes vanish.

Hannah shifted away from Liam, determined not to make a fool of herself.

Liam

Seventeen-year-old Liam Callahan stretched out his long legs beside Hannah, trying to look cool, but inside, his heart was pounding.

He'd compared her to Bree, and yes, Bree was really pretty, but honestly, he couldn't remember the last time he'd seen eyes as deep and dark as Hannah's. Her face was almost perfectly heart shaped, and she wore glossy stuff on her lips that kept drawing his gaze. He desperately tried not to let his eyes drop to her chest, which swelled against the neckline of her cocktail dress, but the effort was causing him to sweat.

Bree hadn't mentioned how pretty her sister was. Liam would have prepared himself better if he'd known.

He thought back to the conversation he'd had with Bree a few days ago after she'd caught him eavesdropping.

"Hear anything interesting while I was talking to Abby about my sister?" Bree had asked, raising her eyebrows.

Embarrassed, Liam had shrugged. "Sorry."

"Actually…" She'd tilted her head to the side and scrunched up her nose, like an idea was forming. "As long as you know about Hannah, you could do me a big favor."

"How?" he'd asked. "What?"

"I'm willing to pay for your time," said Bree, "if you'd be a…well, a date, actually, for my little sister."

Hannah had agreed to come to the wedding, but Bree was concerned that there wouldn't be anyone there that she'd know. It was important to Bree that her sister felt comfortable, and she was hoping that Liam would stick close to her, chat with her, ask her to dance, and make her feel included.

"What do you think?" she'd asked, and Liam could hear the hope in her voice.

He had grimaced. He wanted to help Bree, he really did. But being a blind date to someone's little sister? Someone he'd never met before? It was pretty awkward.

"Yeah…I don't know."

"I'll pay you double whatever Abby pays you!" she'd added.

Hmm. Well, that had made everything more interesting. Abby paid him ten dollars an hour to do chores around the vineyard. At twenty dollars an hour, he'd make a *lot* just for putting on a dress shirt and hanging out with someone's sister at a wedding.

"What time do I need to be there?"

Abby beamed at him. "Saturday. Four o'clock. Reception should be over by ten."

Six hours at twenty bucks an hour? There was no way he could say no. Whoever this little sister was, he'd suck it up and hang out with her. The money was worth it.

Bree had clapped her hands and hugged him,

then gave him a few more details about Hannah. She was a junior in high school, lived in southern Oregon, and was interested in theater, movies, and music.

Immediately, Liam realized that they had one important thing in common: Liam's mom lived in Medford, Oregon, where Liam lived during the school year and attended high school. But that was also where their commonality ended. Sure, he enjoyed going to the movies now and then and listened to whatever was on the radio when he was driving somewhere, but drama and music weren't his interests. No matter. For $120, he'd read up on current movies and prepare himself to be the best date ever.

"So," he said, turning to Hannah as the last of the guests found their seats, "I'm actually from Oregon too."

"Seriously?"

He nodded. "Yeah. Medford. I spend the school year with my mom and summers down here with my dad."

"Cool."

"You're from Brookings, right?"

"Mm-hm," she mumbled, looking straight ahead.

Was she shy? She *seemed* kind of shy, giving

him one-word answers.

Make her feel comfortable, man.

"So, uh, you seen any good movies lately?"

Suddenly she turned to face him, and as she moved, he smelled her perfume. It was light and sweet, and he couldn't help thinking that whatever it was, it was the perfect match for her heart-shaped face.

"Definitely! Did you see *Jurassic World*? It was sorta dumb but super entertaining."

Luckily, he had. "Yeah. I thought it was awesome."

"And I just saw *The Spy Who Dumped Me*. So funny!"

He hadn't seen that one, but he liked this animated side of Hannah. "I missed that one. But *Alpha* comes out on Friday. I'm *definitely* seeing that."

"God! Me too!" she exclaimed. "It looks really intense. But *The Little Mermaid* comes out on Friday too, and I sorta want to see that one first. I can't decide."

"So I guess you like movies, huh?"

She nodded. "Movies and theater. I'm going to double major in drama and English in college. Maybe with a Shakespeare concentration."

"Oh, yeah?"

"Mm-hm. How about you?"

"Teaching," he said. "I want to be a kids' swim coach."

"That's really awesome," she said. She stared at him for an extra second, her lips tilting up in a smile. "You don't hear a lot of guys our age talk about being teachers."

Something important that Hannah didn't know was that swimming—or rather, Coach G—had literally saved Liam's life. Working hard for Coach and committing to a sport he loved had straightened Liam out after he'd found himself on the brink of disaster. Getting a teaching degree so that he could coach other kids was now his dream—his way of paying back the world for giving him another chance.

"I don't know if I'll be good at it, but I'd like to give it a try," he said. "Are you going to be an actress?"

"As if!"

He wasn't sure if she said this because acting didn't appeal to her or because she thought she didn't have the looks for acting, but if the latter was the case, it was the second time she'd bashed her looks in ten minutes, and he didn't like it. In fact, he was about to contradict her when she continued.

"I'm thinking more along the lines of playwriting or…"

"Or what?"

"Teaching. Like you," she said, offering him a shy smile.

"Hey, now, would you look at that?" he teased her. "We both live in Oregon, we both liked *Jurassic World*, and we both want to teach. We sure have a lot in common."

"Yeah, I guess we do." Her cheeks flushed, and she looked away for a moment before her deep brown eyes caught his again. "We have it all figured out, huh?"

Suddenly he had the urge to share something real with her. "I didn't always. I repeated a year of high school," he said softly.

She nodded, giving him a polite smile. "There's nothing wrong with that. It gave you extra time to figure out what you want out of life."

He relaxed, grinning at her, grateful that his little bit of truth hadn't been rejected or ridiculed. "And to know a good thing when it comes along," he added.

Was it his imagination or did she blush again

when he said that? Her pretty face was a little pink in the fading light, matching some of the flowers on her dress.

As Pachelbel's Canon started playing, he nudged her gently with his knee.

"You know, I think we're the only two people here tonight under thirty. Want to be my wedding date, Hannah Giacomina?"

He had a feeling that the grin she gave him wasn't one she was accustomed to, because it spread over her face softly and slowly, like it wasn't used to taking up so much real estate—like maybe it wasn't usually allowed to.

She shrugged, but her eyes sparkled as she answered softly, "Sure. Why not?"

Chapter Two

Hannah

As Bree recited the wedding vows she'd written herself, Hannah's eyes welled with tears because her sister's voice was so certain, so terribly in love. As she sniffled softly, a warm handkerchief was pressed into her hand. Her watery eyes trailed up Liam's arm to his face, where she found him looking down at her with a soft expression. His fingers pressed down on the smooth fabric in her palm, gently letting her know that she wasn't alone.

Thanks, she mouthed.

His lips turned up in a small smile as he put his arm around the back of her chair. Her tummy filled with butterflies as his arm grazed her back, and she took a deep breath, wishing she could calm her racing heart.

As Bree and Todd walked back down the aisle to the traditional "Wedding March," Bree caught Hannah's eye and beamed. It was a good thing Hannah was still holding Liam's handkerchief because her eyes totally welled up again.

"You okay?" asked Liam.

"Sorry I'm such a mess," she said, sniffling as she wiped away more tears.

"Isn't it, like, a rule that all girls cry at weddings?"

"Honestly?" she said, looking up into his blue eyes. "Not me. I don't cry at stuff like this."

"Oh, you're the exception?"

"Usually, yeah." She balled up his handkerchief in her hand. "I—I don't really go for all this, like, undying-true-love-forever-and-ever kind of stuff. It's not my thing."

"Huh." He stared at her, scanning her face as though surprised such a girl existed. "Okay...so what *is* your thing, Hannah Giacomina?"

"My *thing*?"

He nodded. "Unlike every other girl on the planet, you're *not* into true love, so what *are* you into?"

Only one word popped into her head—the most important word in the whole world: "Kindness."

"Is kindness separate from love?" he asked.

She looked away from him, taking a deep breath that made her already-tight dress feel even tighter. "It's safer."

"Safer?"

"If you're kind to people and they're kind to you, you won't get hurt."

He tilted his head to the side. "And love will hurt you?"

Hannah thought about her father—the way he'd left Bree's mother and Bree, the way Bree's mother always looked at Hannah with contempt.

She thought about her mother—specifically, her mother's face at her father's funeral; she hadn't been the same since her husband's passing, and maybe she never would be.

She thought about herself—about the boys she'd liked in the past and how none of them had ever returned her affection. One of them, Chad Simpson, had actually told her "You're super cool, Hannah, but you know, you're not really girlfriend material." His eyes had lingered on her oversized chest for a minute before he'd shrugged awkwardly and walked away from her locker. Tears of shame and humiliation and anger had filled her eyes. She was too fat for a boyfriend. Too fat for love.

After that, no matter how fiercely her heart had longed for a boyfriend, she'd stopped hoping for someone to come along. And she'd stopped hoping for love.

His question lingered in the air between them: *And love will hurt you?*

Yes, thought Hannah. *Yes, it will.*

She looked down at the damp white square in her hand and offered it back to Liam.

"You keep it." His brows were knitted together as he stared down at her.

Hannah tucked the handkerchief in her purse as they stood up, trying to ignore the awesome and confusing feeling of his hand on the small of her back. He led her to the end of the aisle and folded them into the crowd of people forming a line to congratulate Bree and Todd.

"You know, you never answered my question," he said from behind her.

Giovanna. Mom. Me.

"Yes," she said, looking at him over her shoulder. "I think love will hurt you."

"You're serious," he said, his voice surprised and low.

"It's risky and stupid."

"Love," he confirmed in a low voice.

"Yes, love," she said, starting to feel impatient with him. "Bree and I are half-sisters with the same last name. How do you think that happened?"

He shrugged as they moved forward in line. "I assume your father divorced her mom and married yours?"

"Exactly," said Hannah. "How do you think that made Giovanna feel? How do you think it made Bree feel? And my mom? My dad never told her that he was married to someone else. She thought he was available. By the time my mom found out he was married, she was already pregnant with me."

"So it was messy."

"*Really* messy," said Hannah, taking another step forward.

Liam blew out a held breath. "But that was *them*, not *you*. You're just going to sideline yourself because your parents made mistakes?"

Yes, she thought. *That's* exactly *what I'm going to do.*

But to her surprise, the words didn't slip from her

lips strong and true. In fact, she found she couldn't actually say them out loud. They sounded so hopeless, so defeated, so bitter. And standing next to handsome Liam Callahan in line to wish Bree and Todd congratulations, she didn't actually *feel* hopeless, defeated, and bitter.

They stepped forward in small increments, and Liam kept his palm lightly on the small of her back.

"I know something about making mistakes," he said, bending down to speak softly near her ear. "You can always choose a different path for yourself."

A shiver of pleasure ran down her back as his breath brushed the skin behind her ear. She let her eyes flutter closed for a second before whipping them open and berating herself. *You're acting ridiculous, Hannah! He's just being nice! Get yourself together!*

"What about you?" she demanded, leaning away from his hand.

"Me?"

"Your mother lives in Oregon. Your father lives in California. What's the superhappy story of *your* parents?" she snapped.

"You're right," he said, flinching as he lowered his hand from her back. "There's no superhappy story there."

His face fell a little, and Hannah instantly regretted her words. He'd been nothing but nice since the moment she'd met him, and she had no right to lash out at him. She was just so confused by how she felt around him. She wanted to stay cool and strong; she didn't want to warm up to him and end up falling for yet *another* boy who'd never be interested in her. She could feel herself weakening, and it scared her.

"I'm sorry, Liam. I shouldn't have said that. I—I had *no right* to say that."

"It's fine," he said softly. "The truth? My father cheated on my mother with his secretary up in Seattle, where we used to live. My mom divorced him and moved to Oregon with me, and he moved down here with his secretary, Jill, who's now my stepmom. More truth? I was really mad at my parents for a long time." He paused before adding, "Got into some trouble, even."

Huh. Well, that explained why he'd repeated a year of high school.

She could see his embarrassment on his face, and she couldn't bear it. He'd been kind to her, offering her his handkerchief and teasing her about being his date. She needed to make amends.

Reaching out, she placed her hand on his arm,

annoyed with herself that touching him made her breath catch and her heart speed up. She forced herself to keep her hand still and not do something totally embarrassing, like pet him.

"But you turned everything around, didn't you? You told me that the extra year gave you time to figure things out," she said.

Feeling nervous, Hannah wet her lips, her tummy buzzing when his eyes cut to her mouth and lingered there for a moment. When he found her eyes again, his face looked so sad, she felt it in her gut. She wished she could go back in time to the moment before she'd snapped at him.

"Yeah," he said, "but it cost something. To me and my parents. Something I can never get back."

He reached for her hand on his arm.

Oh, God. What are you thinking, Hannah? What are you doing? Why are you still touching him? He doesn't want some fat, depressing girl who doesn't believe in love and yelled at him about his parents touching him!

After they'd exchanged pleasantries with Bree and Todd, he'd probably make some excuse and avoid her for the rest of the evening.

Her heart fell at the thought.

It wasn't like someone as beautiful as Liam Callahan would actually be interested in someone like Hannah in real life, but it felt a little wonderful to imagine spending the reception with him, pretending to be his date—pretending, just for a moment, that she was popular and interesting and pretty enough to attract the attention of someone like him.

Her cheeks flaming with embarrassment, she started to slide her hand off his arm, but suddenly she realized that his hand wasn't pushing her away; it was *seeking* hers. Once found, he laced his fingers through Hannah's deliberately, like he wanted to.

Hannah gulped, willing her fingers to relax, to gently clasp his as he was clasping hers, to let her much smaller palm settle flush against his catcher's mitt of a hand.

When she finally found the courage to look up at him, his eyes were soft and tender.

"Sounds like we both have a little baggage." His lips turned up in the beginning of a smile, and relief coursed through her. "You know, if you believed in true love, we'd be a match made in heaven, Hannah Giacomina."

His grin told her that he was just teasing, but his words made something happen to her heart. Not that she suddenly believed that true love was possible for someone like her, but it felt like the Kevlar around her heart was somehow slipping away. Over the heads of the people in front of her, she caught sight of Bree's brilliantly happy smile, which just seemed to encourage the change happening within her.

"By the way, how does someone who doesn't believe in love become a Shakespeare devotee?" Liam asked, squeezing her fingers lightly. "Aren't all of those plays about true love?"

"A common misconception," she said, warming instantly to the safety of the topic. "If anything, his plays are cautionary tales! *Romeo and Juliet*? They both die in the end. *Antony and Cleopatra*? She commits suicide. *King Lear*? Cordelia is murdered, and her father dies of a broken heart. *Hamlet*? Pretty much *everyone* dies."

"Hey, now," he said, tilting his head to the side. "What about *Much Ado about Nothing*? Everybody falls in love and ends up happily married. Or *The Taming of the Shrew*? Everything works out for them too."

"Wait a second! You know Shakespeare?" she asked, feeling a little bit delighted.

He chuckled. "Don't forget: I repeated my

sophomore year of high school. That was a lot of Shakespeare. Plus, Julia Stiles was smokin' hot in *10 Things I Hate about You*."

"I *love* that movie," said Hannah softly, staring up at him in wonder.

He clasped her hand a little tighter, and she glanced from his eyes to his lips. The top one was lightly peaked, but the bottom one was more pillowed. Both were pink and slightly chapped, and she wondered—

"Please stop," he whispered, his voice gritty and low.

She blinked, swallowing as she looked up at his eyes, which seemed darker than they'd been a moment ago. "S-Sorry."

"It's our turn," he said, looking over her head at Bree and Todd.

Hannah gasped lightly, dropping his hand and turning to her sister.

Liam

Liam was grateful for a moment to compose himself while Hannah and Bree hugged each other.

Dang it, but when he agreed to do this job for Bree—to be her sister's date—he'd never expected to really *like* Hannah. He didn't know exactly what he *had* expected, but she was throwing him for a loop. She was different. Unusual. Sort of like a complicated puzzle, and Liam found himself wanting to put the pieces together, positive that something really amazing would be revealed when he was done.

Though her face was stunning and her long chestnut-colored hair was gorgeous, Hannah wasn't a small girl. But Liam wasn't really attracted to girls who were stick-thin; he liked a girl to look *healthy*—to have curves where girls were *supposed* to have curves. It wasn't a turn-off to him that Hannah was a little bigger. Besides, she looked really pretty in her flowered dress with her long hair curling over her shoulders. She put effort into the way she looked, and coupled with her personality, he found himself, well, interested. *Genuinely* interested—not just because he was being paid.

"Liam!" Bree released Hannah and held out her arms to him. "Thanks so much for coming."

Todd, who worked at I Tri Merli and knew

Liam's dad, winked at Liam before sliding his eyes to Hannah and asking her, "Is this guy bothering you, miss?"

Hannah leaned back, two spots of pink flushing her cheeks. "Um. No! He's just—I mean—"

"Quit flustering my date, Todd," said Liam with a chuckle. "And, hey…congratulations! I think the Giacomina girls are catches."

"No arguments here." Todd snuck a glance at his bride before grinning back at the younger man. "You've been a hard worker this summer, Liam. Staying out of trouble. We're proud of you."

"Yes, sir," answered Liam, his jaw tightening a little.

Todd gestured to the reception tent with a flick of his chin. The band was playing their first song, and the sound of conversation and clinked glasses floated over to them on the breeze.

"Looks like the fun is starting. Enjoy yourselves, you two."

Todd and Bree turned to the next guests waiting to offer their congratulations, and Liam grabbed Hannah's hand again, pulling her toward the tent covered with white lights, where the band was playing some corny song from the 1900s.

"Are you okay?" asked Hannah.

He scrubbed the back of his neck with his free hand. "When you've messed up, it's hard for some people to believe that you won't again."

"People like Todd?"

"He's friends with my dad. He's knows about…stuff," said Liam, changing direction slightly and heading toward a garden path flanked by tiki torches. He liked the way Hannah's hand fit inside his, and he wasn't in a hurry to join the thirtysomethings at the reception. "Hey, want to walk around a little first? I could show you the gardens."

"Sure," answered Hannah. "But you have to tell me what happened with Todd."

Nothing had really happened with Todd. Something had happened two years ago, and Todd knew about it. And frankly, Liam didn't feel like getting into it with Hannah. Not right now. Not when he was just getting to know her.

"Later, okay? Tell me more about you and Shakespeare."

"Okay. Like what?"

"Like when you're going to let me take you out on a date to one of the festival plays in Ashland. It's only twenty minutes from my house. We could—"

She stopped walking on the garden path, her brown eyes wide as she stared up at him. "Are you serious?"

"Sure. Why wouldn't I be? And after the play, let's have dinner so you can explain everything that I missed."

One thing about repeating sophomore year in high school was that Liam had attended the Oregon Shakespeare Festival, OSF, in Ashland two years in a row. He'd seen *Much Ado about Nothing* two years ago and *The Taming of the Shrew* last year. He'd even worked at the festival for a week over spring break, taking tickets. And even though he hadn't understood everything the actors were saying, he'd gotten the gist of the plays and ended up enjoying them.

Hannah was still staring up at him, unsmiling, an inscrutable expression on her face. "I guess I wouldn't mind seeing a play...with a *friend*."

"Hmm," he hummed. "Methinks she missed the part where I said *date*."

Her lips twitched. "I didn't miss it. I just don't think—"

"Please don't interrupt me," he said. "I'm about to have a very deep conversation with myself."

He heard her laugh softly as he ducked under a

weeping willow. The massive tree was so dense he couldn't see her, but he grinned when she parted the pendulous branches and stepped into the cool, dim cavern with him.

He had one hand on his hip and another clutched his chin as he leaned against the trunk of the willow tree, looking over at her.

"Mayhap she doesn't like you," he said in a thick British accent.

He switched positions quickly, putting both hands on his hips and frowning at the tree trunk. "Not like me? Inconceivable!"

His hands went back to his hip and chin. "Dost thou think the lady absurd?"

He looked over at her, raised his eyebrows, then shook his head. "Nay."

She giggled quietly, and with her defenses lowered, she was so pretty, she took his breath away. He had to force himself to keep playing his role.

"Is she heartbroken?" he asked himself.

Liam cocked his head to the side, looking over at her. "Not by a lover. She doesn't believe in love."

Her eyebrows creased for a second, giving her away. She believed in love just as much as every other girl he'd ever known. She was just terrified of it.

"Is she fair?" he asked himself softly, taking a step toward her.

Hannah took a deep breath, staring at him, hope and fear warring in her eyes. Her cheeks flushed as he stared back at her, her hands dropping to the hem of her cocktail dress, which she smoothed nervously.

"Aye," he said, his voice low and soft under the half-light of the setting sun filtering through the willow branches. "Very fair. Very beautiful."

She gasped softly. So softly, Liam almost missed it, but oh, how awesome that he didn't.

"Tell me how she's fair," he said, taking two more steps closer. "Her hair is the color of coffee and her eyes are dark and deep. Her"—he looked meaningfully at her chest and sighed with admiration—"*form* is soft and inviting, and the touch of her hand divine. Yet one room in my lady's house steals my peace, disrupts my thoughts, distracts my—
"

Her lips parted, and she started to whisper, "Which par—"

"It's very rude to interrupt a private conversation," he told her quickly, closing whatever distance was left between them. Now standing toe-to-

toe, only a breath could have fit between his chest and hers.

"Were you going to ask which part of her is so distracting?"

She nodded slowly, holding her breath as she stared up at him.

He dropped the accent, reaching up to cup her cheeks, his eyes searching hers. "I have no choice but to show you."

He leaned slightly closer to her. A tiny whimper escaped from her throat as he bent his head, closing the distance between her face and his.

"Here," he whispered, dropping his lips to hers.

Chapter Three

Liam

When Liam first ducked under the willow tree, it was mostly to conceal the disappointment he'd felt when Hannah had dropped his hand and called him a friend, but he could see her loosening up as he continued his silly, pseudo-Shakespearean soliloquy, so he'd kept on going.

And though stealing a kiss from her hadn't been his goal when he started, as her face grew softer and her eyes dilated to almost black, he couldn't help himself.

Her lips were soft and slightly parted as he brushed them with his, his thumb lightly stroking her cheek as she sighed into his mouth.

As he drew back, her eyes opened slowly and her

lips turned up in a surprised smile.

"*So* distracting," he murmured, staring at her pretty face.

The flush in her cheeks deepened as her tongue darted out to wet her lips. "I didn't expect that."

"I didn't plan it."

She bit her bottom lip, and it took every ounce of willpower in his seventeen-year-old body not to kiss her again.

"Things like this don't happen to me," she whispered. "Like, ever."

"Me neither," he confessed.

She scoffed. "You're a hot swimmer. I highly doubt that."

He flexed his pecs and grinned at her. "You think I'm hot?"

Her already-flushed cheeks deepened to crimson, and she looked down at the ground, mumbling. "Oh, God. Shoot me now."

"Hannah," he said, chuckling softly when she looked up at him with a huge wince. "I wasn't kidding before. I think you're beautiful."

She didn't say anything—just stared at him, her brown eyes uncertain but pleased.

"Okay," he said, dropping his hands from her

warm face but grabbing her hand so he could keep touching her. "I guess we should actually *attend* the reception, since Bree's your sister and all."

Her face relaxed into a grin. "If we don't, she'll think you abducted me."

"That's not such a bad idea," he joked.

Hannah laughed, pulling him toward the edge of the willow branches, and the sound of her laughter was so awesome, Liam had to physically restrain himself from drawing her back into the quiet darkness beneath the boughs and kissing her again.

His heart was slowing down now, but he was so *aware* of it—of the way it had swelled and hammered when he'd kissed her. He'd only known her for an hour or so...how had she gotten under his skin so fast?

Because she was pretty? Sure, that was a part of it, but not enough for him to make a move on her so quickly.

Because they were at a wedding? Yeah, that was part of it too. Rules—especially rules for romance— were relaxed at weddings.

But it was more than that, he realized, as they walked side by side down the tiki-torch-lit path. It was because she felt hopeless about love, and Liam knew what it was to feel hopeless about life, and he didn't want her to feel that way.

He glanced at her dark hair, the way it fanned out over her shoulders, and it occurred to him that while she projected hopelessness in order to protect herself, she really *wasn't* hopeless. Not really. Not deep down inside, where it mattered. She said she didn't believe in true love, but he saw the way she cried at the wedding, the way she looked at Todd and Bree in the receiving line, the way she let him hold her hand and kiss her under the weeping willow. She was scared— hell, *terrified*—of love. She had a right to her fears, after the way her father had treated his first wife and her half-sister. But hopeless? No. She wasn't. She just *wished* she was.

And all Liam wanted to do was prove to her that she didn't need to be so scared.

It was dark as they walked hand in hand up the garden pathway toward the big white tent covered in white twinkle lights.

"So, date," he said, "how are you at dancing?"

"Not great," she answered glumly.

"If I lead, will you follow?"

"Maybe," she answered, "but there's just as good a chance I'll step on your toes."

"My toes are pretty tough," he reassured her.

"Are *you* a good dancer?" she asked.

No, he thought, *but it's such a nice excuse to have you in my arms.*

"I guess."

"You don't sound so sure."

He stopped walking and gave her a look. "You hold on to someone and sway. It's not that hard, Hannah Banana."

"Hannah...Banana? Banana!" She pursed her lips and shook her head at him. "Oh no. That's not going to stick. Absolutely not."

"It's either that or Mina."

"Why 'Mina'?"

"From Giacomina," he said. "All the guys on the swim team have nicknames. I'm into them right now."

"What's yours?" she challenged.

"Let me call you Mina."

"Mina." She rolled her eyes, but a grin wasn't far behind, and she looked super cute as she bit her bottom lip, considering the nickname. "Okay, fine. You can call me Mina. Now, tell me your nickname. Is it Lee?"

"Please, no," he groaned. "I feel like a first

grader when someone calls me that."

"Well, no one would mistake you for one." She gave him a saucy look, flicking her eyes to his broad chest, then back up to his face.

"Do that again and I'll drag you back to the willow tree."

She giggled, and it sounded like music in his ears. "Okay. Not Lee. Cal? From Callaghan?"

He took a deep breath. "Otter."

"Otter?" she exclaimed, giggling harder.

"Otter. Like the superfast swimming mammal."

"Swimming *rodent*."

"You love giving me crap!" He laughed, shaking his head. "The guys love saying things like 'We otter let Otter go first' or 'You otter bring a hot date tonight, Otter.' It's ridiculous. You're not going to call me that, are you?"

"I might," she teased.

"You don't like Liam?"

Her kissable lips tilted up in a lovely smile. "I like Liam very much."

And there is was again—that feeling of his heart swelling and hammering from the sweetness of her words.

"Hey, you know what?" he asked. "You didn't

let me finish my pitch before, when I asked you to go on a date with me."

She sighed, her eyes losing a little brightness and her smile dimming as she turned away to look at the reception guests on the dance floor. He tilted his head to see her better, and though he didn't know her well enough to read her expression with accuracy, he saw wariness as her eyebrows knitted together. But when she sucked her lower lip into her mouth, he perceived a little bit of longing too, which made him press his advantage.

"Didn't you wonder how I knew all that Shakespeare stuff?" he asked.

"Yes, actually," she said, looking surprised by his question. "Come to think of it, I did wonder, but then you distracted me."

He grinned. "*Good* distraction, right?"

She rolled her eyes, but her lips tilted up a little, which made him happy. "You were saying?"

"The OSF is close to my house, so if you'd like to go with me sometime—*as a date*—I might even be able to take you backstage. I'm sure Julia would give us a tour of the Allen Elizabethan Theatre."

"Julia?" said Hannah, raising an eyebrow.

He saw it in her eyes, the way she was mentally

backing away from him at the mere mention of another woman. Is that how she saw all men? As players? As someone who'd hurt her and cheat on her if she let her guard down? He couldn't help the way his feelings for her surged as he watched her—how much he wanted to be the person to prove to her that she could give her heart to someone who would keep it safe.

"*Julia* is my mom's friend who works in group sales, is married, and has two kids." He pulled Hannah's hand behind his back, holding it hostage and drawing her closer until her chest pressed against his. "And to be clear? I wouldn't ask you out if I was seeing someone else. I don't do that. I'm not with anyone right now, Hannah…except you."

She flinched, and her face went utterly blank, except for her eyes, which looked worried and uncomfortable.

"You're *not* with me," she said softly, loosening her hand from his grasp and stepping away from him.

"I didn't mean—"

"I have to use the ladies' room. I'll find you in a little bit, okay?"

She turned and started walking away while he babbled incoherently at her back: "Wait. Hannah! No,

I didn't…I just—I just meant…Crap!"

He stopped talking when she was out of sight.

Dang it, Liam! Why do you have to be so freaking intense?

Probably because it bothered him that she kept trying to friend-zone him when he didn't feel *friendly* toward her and pretty much hadn't from the moment he'd laid eyes on her.

There were some girls he met—especially the shallow, self-absorbed ones—who turned him off the moment he met them. Most of the popular girls at his high school thought he was trouble, and even after he'd straightened himself out, they didn't give him a chance. Not really. They'd fool around with him at a party—there was never a shortage of popular girls who wanted to make out with a bad boy—but on Monday morning, they'd act like they'd been too drunk to remember kissing him. And it sort of sucked, because Liam Callahan was one of those guys who quietly longed for a girlfriend, even though his reputation had pegged him inaccurately as a player.

He wanted to date someone. He wanted to leave a party with her on Saturday night and hold her hand when he walked into school on Monday morning. He wanted to be the first person she texted when she was happy or upset about something. He wanted to invite her over for dinner with his mom. He wanted to introduce her to his friends.

You guys, this is my girlfriend.

He'd *imagined* saying those words about a thousand times, but he'd never had the chance to say them, and it bothered him. A lot.

But tonight? Meeting Hannah? Somehow it felt like maybe what he wanted was actually, *finally*, possible. When Hannah looked up at him with those huge, vulnerable, dark-brown eyes, he felt idiotically hopeful.

"Damn it," he growled softly, frustrated that he'd pushed her too hard.

Maybe he was being pushy, but he liked her, and for all he knew, she was driving back up to Brookings in the morning. He wanted her to say yes to a date— his heart needed to *know* that he'd see her again.

Catching sight of the open bar, he walked over and was about to order a stiff drink when he heard Coach G's voice in his head: *Your body's your temple. Treat it right.*

"What can I get you?" asked the bartender.

"Ginger ale, please."

He hated it that his eyes gravitated toward the

direction where Hannah had beelined in search of the bathroom. Would she come back? Or would she avoid him for the rest of the evening?

Be cool, Liam. Be way cooler.

Liam stalked out of the tent, back into the darkness, wondering when *and if* he'd see Hannah again.

Hannah

As she walked to the bathroom, Hannah rubbed her arms, feeling uncharacteristically cold, and tried to get her riot of emotions under control.

She liked Liam.

No, she hadn't known him for very long, but she liked him.

A lot.

She liked the way he'd sat next to her at the ceremony, offering her his handkerchief and teasing her out of tears. She liked their easy banter and the way her hand felt small in his because Hannah never felt small.

But she didn't like the way her heart had started free-falling the second she met him. She didn't like the way he made her hope and wonder and wish. She didn't like the way she was risking her heart just by holding his hand in the dusky light as they walked around the beautiful gardens at I Tri Merli. She didn't like the way he made her long for things that would only hurt her in the long run.

Staring at herself in the mirror of the small powder room on the second floor of the vineyard tasting room, she had a feeling she wasn't supposed to be up here. Restrooms for the guests were clearly marked on the ground floor, but she needed a quiet moment to figure out what the heck was going on and give herself a stern talking-to, so she'd poked around a bit until she found this quiet room at the end of a dimly lit corridor. She sat on a small, fussy stool at a vanity table, probably meant for brides checking their faces before heading downstairs to say "I do."

For a moment she imagined herself in a white veil with her brown hair falling in waves down her back, but the fantasy only lasted for a moment before she grimaced at her reflection. She wouldn't look tiny and perfect like Bree. She'd look like a big fat marshmallow.

"Get real, Hannah," she said to her reflection. "Stop wanting things you can't have."

From the moment she'd locked eyes with Liam Callahan, she'd been throwing caution to the wind, and while a stolen kiss could be forgiven at an event as romantic as a wedding, Hannah wasn't behaving like herself, which bothered her most of all. She didn't hold hands with people she didn't know or kiss strange boys under weeping willows. She was more careful and practical than that. And yet every time she turned around, there he was, offering her a teasing smile or looking at her like she wasn't size-sixteen Hannah Giacomina. And she had to admit…it felt a little bit awesome.

She took a deep breath, reapplying her lip gloss as she looked at her face in the mirror and tried to see herself through a stranger's eyes.

"Okay. You have a pretty face," she said aloud, tilting her head to the side. *Which part of her is so distracting?* Hannah pursed her shiny lips together, remembering the way it felt to be kissed by Liam, and it occurred to her that although it scared her to spend more time with him, she really didn't want to push him away either.

Could she find the courage to believe that this

crazy-cute boy was interested in her? Oh, she would be careful not to expect anything serious or long term. She bet that by tomorrow, when he had a lot more choices than the other nonexistent teens at this wedding, he wouldn't be interested in her anymore. But for now, for tonight, there was no one but her. Besides, she liked him. Maybe she could just allow herself to enjoy it while it lasted?

"Okay. But don't you dare get attached," she warned herself with a stern look. "You're just having fun, not looking for love."

She pushed her shoulders back and her chest forward, glancing at her face again and smiling. Then she grabbed her purse and headed back downstairs.

Standing at the edge of the tent, she scanned the open-air ballroom for a glimpse of him, but he was nowhere in sight, so she crossed over to the nearest bar.

"What can I get you?" asked the bartender.

"Diet Coke, please."

"And you, sir?" he asked, looking over her shoulder.

"Another ginger ale."

Hannah turned at the sound of Liam's voice, unable to keep herself from beaming because she was so danged happy to be next to him again.

Liam's face transformed immediately from closed and uncertain to surprised and pleased. "Hey, you."

"Hi," she said, a little bit dazzled by the wattage of his smile.

"Didn't know if you were coming back."

"Truth? Me neither."

"Glad you decided to give me another chance."

The bartender cleared his throat, and Liam reached around Hannah to take their drinks, his arm brushing her shoulder as he handed her a wineglass filled with soda.

"Listen," she said and took a sip from the straw. "Could we forget about everything else and just have fun tonight? What do you think?"

He raised his glass and clanked hers gently. "To fun."

She grinned back at him. "To fun."

Chapter Four

Liam

They danced several times and cheered loudly, sitting side by side at their assigned table, when Bree and Todd cut the cake. As the evening progressed, Hannah loosened up, smiling more and brooding less, and every minute that went by, Liam liked her more and more.

The drunken—and fortyish—wedding guest seated beside Hannah kept staring at her chest, and two hours into the reception, Liam was fighting against his temper, ready to punch the guy in the face if Hannah indicated that she was feeling uncomfortable.

"Ignore him," said Hannah.

"I'm trying," Liam growled.

"Oh, wait!" she said. "I have an idea. Play along, okay?" She tapped the guy on the arm and said, "I don't think you've met my husband, Liam."

Surprised as hell, Liam forced himself not to laugh as he held out his hand to the old letch, who shook it sloppily. He put his other arm around Hannah's shoulders, loving the way she leaned back against him.

"I'm Liam. Mina's husband."

The gross old guy narrowed his eyes, his head swaying on his neck. "Who t' hell's Mina?"

"I am," said Hannah.

"No. No, no, nnnnnope," the man insisted, poking a wobbly finger at her. "Yer *Hannah*. Hannah, Hannah, Hannah…"

Liam cleared his throat. "Pardon me, but I think I know my wife's name."

"You two…yer just—yer con-confusin' me! On purpose!" The man swayed in his seat, staring at Hannah's breasts for a long time before looking up at Liam. "Y'say yer her husband, huh?"

"That's right." Liam clenched his jaw, just daring the guy to say something inappropriate.

"Lucky bastard."

Hannah gasped in surprise, but Liam laughed, tightening his hand around her shoulder. "Right again."

"You seem—seem awful young t'me," the man said, hiccupping loudly and wobbling in his seat.

"There's no stopping true love," Liam replied. "When you know, you know."

Hannah widened her eyes at him over her shoulder, but she also grinned like he was adorable, so Liam counted it as a win. He bent his neck so that his lips were a breath away from her ear.

"Getting hitched was *your* idea," he whispered.

Did she realize that she'd leaned her head slightly to the side, giving him perfect access to the soft, warm skin of her throat? He forced himself not to drop his lips to her neck, remembering that if he wanted a chance for something *real* with her, moving too fast tonight wasn't going to help his cause. The end goal wasn't just making out with her. The end goal was still knowing her tomorrow.

"Dance with me, wife," he murmured, noticing the way her body readjusted just slightly against him as though she shivered or trembled from his words. He raised his voice, looking at the man. "Going to dance with my bride now."

"D-Damn kids gettin' married"—he hiccupped—"all over the…damn place."

Liam stood up and offered his hand to Hannah, who took it, letting him help her to her feet. As they walked onto the dance floor, he realized for the first time that the crowd was starting to thin out. He glanced at his watch. Ten to eight. The reception would be over soon.

Just as they reached the floor, the music switched from an upbeat song to the Beatles' "In My Life."

He held her hand a little tighter, pulling her close and placing his other hand on her lower back as they found a spot on the edge of the floor. Looking into her eyes felt too intense, so he broke eye contact, looking over her shoulder but leaning so close that her hair brushed against his cheek. Where her hand rested on his back, just over his shoulder, he felt the heat of her palm through his shirt.

After a few notes, she inhaled, her chest pushing against his, and he leaned back to look at her, searching her eyes with wonder and thinking that if she kept looking at him like that, he'd have no choice. He'd be forced to kiss her again. He wouldn't be able to help himself.

But just then, as though she'd read his mind, she

glanced down, staring at his shoulder, so he leaned his head forward again, smelling the sweetness of her hair against his cheek. Her fingers moved on his back, stroking, kneading absently, and it was so distracting and so nice, he drew back to look into her eyes again.

When she bit her bottom lip, his breath caught, but he caught sight of Todd watching them from across the dance floor, so he spun her gently under his arm, which won him a small grin and broke the tension between them for a moment.

Friends and lovers.

As she folded back into his arms, he didn't extend their hands but pulled them close to his chest, still laced together. And after her hand landed back on his shoulder, she slid it up to his neck, her fingers finding his skin over the collar of his shirt as she nestled closer to him.

No one like you.

His breath caught from the incredible feeling of holding her so close, and he dropped her hand to wrap his arms around her waist and pull her flush against his body. His heart skipped a beat when her other hand skated up his arm to his back, tentatively clasping her other hand on his neck, lacing together against his skin—pulling him to her, not pushing him away.

Memories lose meaning.

Their feet barely moved at all now as they swayed slowly back and forth, their shallow breathing pressing their bodies into each other as the soft music played on. Liam clenched his jaw against the rush of his feelings, leaning down to nuzzle her ear with his nose as her forehead rested in the curve of his neck and her breath fanned the skin of his throat.

And love is new.

He wasn't ready to say good night to her, let alone good-bye. He didn't want tonight to end. Not here. Not yet. She was holding him, her thumbs sending shivers down his back as they dusted back and forth across his skin in time to the music. She was *holding* him, and more important, she was *letting* him hold her.

He drew back again to look at her, and her eyes were dark and drowsy, staring at his lips, and he gazed back at her, knowing she could feel his ragged breath against her face.

"Hannah," he murmured. He was desperate not to break the moment, but he also was afraid to kiss her in public, no matter how much he wanted to. "What are you doing after this?"

She wet her lips, finally looking away from his mouth and into his eyes. "After?"

He nodded. "Where are you staying tonight?"

"Bree's place."

"Do you, um…" He didn't want to push her by inviting himself over. He wanted it to be her idea. "Do you want me to drive you?"

"Yes," she whispered quickly, glancing back at his lips again.

"You're killing me," he groaned.

His words, delivered like a plea, seemed to break the spell she was under just enough so that she took a deep breath and looked around to find her sister. "We should say good-bye first."

"Mmm," he murmured, leaning forward again to brush her cheek with his. "Wait till the song's over."

She relaxed in his arms, dropping her head to his shoulder, and suddenly Liam wished the song would never end. He didn't know exactly what was happening between them or what would happen at her sister's house—let alone what would happen after they said good-bye. But holding her felt better than anything he could remember, and after being her constant companion for the last four hours, he couldn't imagine watching her walk away. He could barely imagine letting her out of his arms.

When the song ended, they swayed back and forth for an extra moment before she loosened her hands from around his neck and leaned back, looking up at him with a sad smile. Regretfully, he unclasped his hands and let them skim from her back to her waist, where they lingered for a moment before he pulled them away.

"Say good-bye?" he asked.

Her brows knitted together. "But I thought you were going to drive me—"

"To Bree and Todd, not to each other."

"Oh." She exhaled, laughing softly. "Right."

And if he hadn't kissed her under the willow tree or just danced with her like they were falling in love, then watching her face in that moment would have been the best part of his entire evening. Because it told him something that rocked his world and gave him hope: she wasn't ready to walk away from him either.

Hannah

As Liam pulled into traffic, Hannah glanced over at him.

Was all of this real? Or was it just some beautiful dream she'd wake from at any moment?

Trying to convince herself that they were "just having fun" was getting tougher as the evening progressed, and she knew the smart thing would have been to say good night after the reception and go their separate ways. But the idea of saying good-bye to him was strangely unbearable.

Growing up an only child, chunky, supershy Hannah had been ripe for teasing from the get-go, and short of being bullied outright, she had certainly been the target of more than one pulled pigtail. By junior high, she always had her nose in a book, and her lack of athleticism contributed to a more rounded shape than most of the other preadolescent girls. And so the teasing had continued…especially when her breasts and butt became her roundest parts of all.

By high school, teasing was exchanged for a different kind of attention: Hannah had become attractive to some of the same boys who used to call her Titanic Tits or Bookworm Boobs. She'd watch as their eyes dropped to the front of her shirt and widen with wonder. But their reactions to her developing body made Hannah more uncomfortable and distrustful than ever. The same boys who'd ridiculed her were now interested in her? She avoided them as much as possible, secretly longing for a boyfriend who would see her *heart*, who would like her for who she was. And until then, it was easier to believe that love was just a pretty myth.

When Liam had mentioned *The Taming of the Shrew* and *Much Ado about Nothing*, Hannah had flinched inwardly, recollecting the happily-ever-afters at the ends of both plays. For all her protestations about true love—for as much as she'd tried to convince herself that she wasn't interested in her own happily-ever-after—she longed for a boyfriend, yearned to fall head over heels for someone. Someone who loved her curves *and* her brains, someone who would make her want to say yes instead of no when he put his hands on her body, someone who would make her laugh and see life from a different angle and try new things. But most of all, someone she could trust. Until she found someone she could trust, Hannah simply wouldn't allow herself to fall.

"Next left?" Liam asked.

She started, surprised to hear him speak after

riding in silence for so long. "Mm-hm."

His profile was chiseled and handsome in the dim light of the car, and she stared at him for an extra second. Could Liam possibly be that someone? Was there even the remotest chance that she could meet a boy at her sister's wedding and he could somehow turn out to be someone special in her life? Her heart leaped, whispering a hopeful *maybe*.

"So, will, um, Bree and Todd be home tonight?"

"No," said Hannah. "They're staying in a suite at the Vintner's Inn tonight."

"Oh. So you're..."

"Staying on my own. Bree didn't want me to have to pay for a hotel room," she added nervously.

"You don't mind?"

"Staying alone? No, not at all. There's twenty-four-hour security patrol. Plus, I'm sort of excited to have a whole apartment to myself tonight."

As soon as the words left her mouth, she regretted them. While she *had* looked forward to having the apartment all to herself when Bree had first suggested it, she realized it sounded like she didn't want him to hang out for a while. And though it made her nervous to think of being alone with him, she definitely didn't want him to go.

"Oh," he said softly. "Then I'll just make sure you get there safely."

She sat miserably beside him as he turned, braking at the stoplight at the end of Bree's street. Damn, but she wasn't good with boys. She wasn't smooth. Never had been. And mustering the courage to invite him to come inside suddenly seemed insurmountable.

Liam

"Which number again?" Liam asked, his hopes for spending more time with her dwindling as they approached Bree's apartment. Hannah couldn't have been more clear: she was looking forward to a night alone.

"Thirty-two," she answered.

He slowed down, pulling into the marked parking space. He glanced at Hannah, who wasn't exactly hurrying to leave, and he felt an intense awkwardness settle between them. There was really nothing else he could do. He'd asked her out twice, and twice she'd been evasive. He'd offered her a ride home, but she hadn't taken it a step further to invite him inside. As much as he liked her, as much as he wanted to follow her inside her sister's apartment to find out what would happen next between them, it was her move.

She looked up at him with those big, worried eyes, and he made one small decision: he put the car in park and cut the engine.

As silence overtook them, she looked down and took a deep breath, holding it for several seconds, like maybe she was counting to ten or gathering up her courage to say something. When she looked up, her cheeks were pink in the parking lot lights, but there was a determined glint in her eyes as she asked, "Liam, um, I was wondering if…I mean, do you want to—"

"Yes."

"Phew," she said, her shoulders sagging with relief.

He didn't want to give her a chance to change her mind. "Wait there."

He exited the car, rounded it quickly, then opened her door and offered her his hand. And when she placed it in his—where, frankly, he was starting to believe it *belonged*—all the awkwardness of the drive home slipped away.

She stood up, and he felt so happy that she wasn't saying good night or good-bye, he put his hands on her waist and drew her close. She stared up at him, flattening her hands on his chest, which flexed automatically under her palms. Man, he liked her.

"I want to kiss you again," he said. "Ever since we danced, I—"

"Me too."

Caught off guard by her quick yes, he smiled at her, flicking his eyes to her lips, which she parted softly in invitation. Dipping his head, he caught the bottom one, holding it between his for a moment before tilting his head to seal his lips over hers more fully. She whimpered, and her fingers curled into his shirt as he touched his tongue to hers. He tightened his arms around her, and she ran her hands up his chest until they circled his neck, as they had when they were dancing, and Liam groaned into her mouth because while they'd danced, all he'd thought about was kissing her. All he'd wanted *then* was *this*. And now, by some miraculous stroke of luck, his fantasy was coming true.

"Hannah, Hannah, Hannah," he mumbled softly, kissing her cheek and her jawbone and the soft skin of her neck that she'd bared to him at the table when he had teasingly called her his wife.

"Let's go inside," she said, letting her hands part and skim down his arms as she stared at his neck. She cleared her throat. "Liam, I just…I mean, I want you to come in, but we just met each other, and I'm not the sort of girl who—"

"Look at me," he demanded in a low, serious voice. "Nothing's going to happen unless you want it to. You understand?"

She nodded.

"I promise, Hannah. The second you say no to anything, we stop. Okay?"

She nodded, tilting her head to the side. "I'm so glad I met you tonight."

"Not as glad as I am. You're the first girl I've met in a long time who…" He was about to say "who I can actually see myself falling for" but stopped himself. If he'd said it, he would have meant it, but it felt like too much too soon, and he didn't want to scare her away again.

"Who…what?" she asked, brown eyes luminous.

He dropped his hands from around her and gestured to the metal gate that opened into the apartment complex courtyard. She pulled a keycard from her purse and held it up to the reader. Following behind her, Liam scrambled to come up with a plausible way to finish the sentence that wouldn't have her running for the hills.

"Who what, Liam?" she asked again, softer this time, over her shoulder.

"Who I've wanted to ask out on a date." They were walking around a luminescent aqua-blue pool and she stopped, turning around to look at him. He did his best to look pitiful. "And you won't even say yes."

She rolled her eyes, then turned back around and kept walking toward her sister's apartment.

"I won't give up, Hannah," he said to her back. "Just so you know? My goal by the end of tonight is for you to say yes. 'Yes, Liam, I would love to see you again.'"

Hannah stopped at a bright-orange door and held the keycard up to the reader, waiting until the light turned green. Then she turned the knob and opened the door, flicking a switch in the doorway to flood the hallway with soft light.

"We'll see," she said, stepping inside.

For Liam, it was a small but significant victory. For the first time since he'd started asking her out tonight, she didn't flinch or run to the bathroom or try to slap in him the friend-zone. Progress. *I'll take it.*

"Want a soda?" she asked, placing her purse on a table by the door and turning left into the kitchen.

"Sure," he answered, continuing down the hallway into Bree's living room.

He wasn't surprised to find that, like Bree, it was warm and homey. Knickknacks, framed photos, and tons of books lined shelves flanking an electric fireplace. A flowered couch looked plush and comfortable, and a pair of slippers waited by a cozy leather chair.

Hannah joined him, offering him a glass bottle of Coke and holding one of her own.

"This is the good stuff," he said.

"Yes," she said, her wide eyes sparkling. "It is."

Aw, Hannah, what you do to my heart.

"What are we drinking to?" he asked.

"Umm." She took a deep breath, and her face softened just a little. "Shakespeare's plays?"

"How about we drink to seeing one together?"

She didn't say anything, but he saw the slight trace of a smile as she raised her bottle to touch his before putting it between her lips. He stared, transfixed, as she settled her lips around the head of the bottle and tipped it back—it was so unintentionally sexy, he couldn't have looked away if he tried, and his whole body tightened.

When she lowered the bottle, she grinned at him as if she knew exactly what he was thinking. "I'm going to throw on some jeans."

He nodded, reaching for his tie. "Mind if I lose the tie and jacket?"

"Go for it," she said. "You know, there's a fire pit out by the pool. Are you any good at making fires?"

"I think I could generate a little heat," he said, winking at her. "Meet me out there?"

She nodded before slipping into a dark back hallway. Liam placed his tie and jacket on the arm of the couch, grinning to himself as it occurred to him: when he'd asked her to see a play with him, she hadn't said no.

Chapter Five

Liam

After pulling two lounge chairs from the pool over to the fire pit area, he gathered an armful of available logs from a pile by the fence and built a fire, tepee style.

Hmm. So she wasn't saying no to a date anymore, but she still hadn't said yes, and Liam couldn't help but wonder if maybe she didn't trust him. After all, he'd alluded to a "checkered past," but he hadn't come clean with her about what had happened.

And then he remembered something his mother was fond of saying: "If you want someone's trust, offer them your honesty."

Looking up, he saw Hannah walking over from

her sister's apartment, wearing jeans and a loose-fitting gray sweater. Her hair was down, and her feet were bare, and she looked so natural and casual and pretty, she made his heart ache.

He lit the fire and stayed squatting beside it as Hannah took the lounger directly behind him. Once the fire had caught, he swiveled to look up at her.

"Why won't you go out with me?" he asked directly. "Is it because of my past? Because I told you I got into trouble and needed to repeat a year?"

Her eyebrows knitted together, and she shook her head quickly. "No. Not at all, Liam. Gosh, I hate it that you even wondered that."

He stood up and sat down on the middle of the lounger beside her, facing her. He didn't know if he believed her or not, even though she sounded genuine. She was a nice person, and in his experience, nice people said what you wanted to hear, even if it wasn't 100 percent how they felt.

Suddenly something occurred to him, and it made his stomach drop like he'd swallowed a boulder. Maybe Todd had pulled her aside at the reception and told her about his past. Maybe she already knew what had happened. Maybe she'd never say yes to seeing him again because she thought he was too screwed up.

His frustration mounted.

"I think it's hard for people to give second chances, to believe that someone can really change, but I promise you, I have."

She shifted her body, lying on her side, her pretty face looking at him. "It's not you, it's me."

"Oh, okay," he said sarcastically. "I've never heard that one before."

"What does that mean?"

"It means nice girls don't date guys who got busted for drugs."

She gasped. "Whoa! What?" Her lips parted in shock as she stared unblinkingly at him. "I had no idea—I mean, I didn't know you—"

"I thought maybe Todd told you."

She gulped, her eyes wide and concerned as she shook her head. "No! He didn't say anything. I promise."

Liam winced at her expression, wondering if he was doing the right thing but desperately needing to come clean to her. "Can I tell you what happened? Can I be honest with you?"

She stared back at him, saying nothing, her eyes scanning his face like she was trying to process what he'd just said.

"Please, Hannah," he insisted. "Please, can I tell you what happened?"

"Yeah," she whispered. "Tell me."

Liam took a deep breath, resting his sweaty hands on his knees.

"I thought we were a happy family," he started softly, searching her eyes as he started telling his story. "I mean, we weren't perfect, but as far as I could tell, my parents loved each other, and I always felt sure they loved me. And suddenly it all came crashing down. My dad cheats on my mom with his secretary. My mom divorces him. She and I move to Oregon to be closer to her sister, and my dad and Jill, his secre—um, new wife—move here. So there I was in a new city, and I didn't know anyone in school. And it wasn't exactly easy to make friends two-thirds of the way through freshman year."

"I can imagine," she said, her voice warm, though her eyes were still cautious.

"I was alone. Really, really alone."

"I know," she said softly, nodding at him to continue.

"I literally had one friend. One. Theo. And he had an older brother, Rob, who hung out with this—I don't know how to put it—group of guys, I guess…but they were rough, you know? Not a gang, but really rough. Drinking, smoking pot. Knocking over mailboxes. Spray-painting graffiti on overpasses. They'd all been busted for destruction of property and stuff like that. Sometimes when I was over at Theo's place, we'd see them, but I'd cut out of there…mostly because they made me nervous.

"So, anyway, the summer after freshman year, my mom went back to work as the dispatcher at the local police station, where she worked really irregular hours. And I…" He shook his head back and forth, dropping her eyes. "I hung out at Theo's all summer because I didn't—I don't know…I guess I didn't feel like I had anywhere else to go, and being home alone was too depressing, you know?

"One day we're playing X-Box, and one of guys comes into the den and asks Theo to take a backpack to the mall. Rob steps in and says Theo can't because he has 'stuff to do,' so the guy—his name was Spider—looks at me and asks me to do it. And I—I don't know what I was thinking. I was stupid. I wanted to fit in. And I was sort of scared of saying no. So I took the backpack, and I didn't ask what was in it. I was like, *I'll just get it over with. I'll take it to the mall, drop it off and go home.*

"I rode my bike to the mall and sat down at a table in the food court with the backpack like they told me to—it was bright red with a big spider drawn on it in black Sharpie. Anyway, I put it on the table and waited for a girl named Tina to come and get it.

"Five minutes later, I'm surrounded by police and facedown on the ground. Turned out it was heavy because there was a kilo of cocaine in the bottom of the bag and books on top of the package. 'Tina' was an undercover cop named Martina Alessio who'd been trying to bust Spider for months."

He looked up to meet her eyes and flinched at the compassion and kindness he saw there. She didn't speak, and she didn't reach for him. She pillowed her hands under her head and listened quietly as he told his story.

Even though it was s shameful story about a scared and lonely kid, it was a part of who he was, and Liam needed to own it in order to reassure her that it was in his past.

"I never used cocaine. I never tried it. I'd never even seen what it looked like before that day. I swear. But I was arrested for juvenile drug possession with intent to distribute."

"At fourteen," she murmured.

He nodded. "At fourteen."

Hannah took a deep breath and rolled to her back, staring up at the night sky, and it was like a hit to his chest to watch her pull away. So he'd been right after all; she didn't want to date him because of his troubled history.

While he understood where she was coming from, there was nothing he could do about it. Yes, he'd been arrested. He couldn't change what had happened, and if his past was a deal breaker for her, he may as well say good-bye to her now before he embarrassed himself any further.

"Well, thanks for listening. I, uh, I guess…I'll get going."

"No!" She sat up, swinging her legs over the side of the lounger so her knees touched his. "Don't go. It's okay. It was a mistake."

He swallowed, blinking against a sudden and intense burn of tears.

She reached out, taking one of the hands on his lap and lacing her fingers through his.

"Tell me the rest."

Looking down at their entwined fingers made him feel so profoundly grateful for second chances, it knocked the wind out him, and for a moment he couldn't speak. All he could do was squeeze her fingers gently, feeling thankful that he'd met her.

When he finally looked up at her, her brown eyes were dark and shiny in the firelight, full of tenderness and understanding.

"Hannah," he murmured, his heart swelling almost painfully as her lips turned up in the smallest, gentlest smile he'd ever seen.

Until that moment, he'd never seen anything or anyone as beautiful as Hannah Giacomina. And in that moment, he knew that he was falling for her more deeply than he'd ever thought possible in such a short amount of time. It overcame him and encouraged him, terrified him that something he'd wanted for so long might actually be happening right before his eyes and that somehow, some way, Hannah might give him the chance that no other girl had.

"It's okay," she whispered again as the fire crackled and snapped beside them, shooting bright-orange sparks into the sky. "Tell me the rest of your story."

He swallowed, and his voice was shaky and emotional as he continued. "My mom had started dating this cop, Brian, in August, and when I was booked, he was off duty, but she called him to come in. He was furious, and she was crying, and it was the first time I really realized how much trouble I was in.

"My mom found a lawyer, but she had to call my dad to ask him to pay for it, and he came up and read me the riot act once I was released to the care of my mother. I mean, I was fourteen years old, facing juvenile detention, and I was scared. Oh, my God, Hannah, I was so scared.

"My mom and Brian tried to force me to tell the police who'd given me the backpack, but I wouldn't. No matter what, I wouldn't mention Theo, Rob, or Spider. It's not that I wanted to stay friends with them—I stayed away from Theo after what happened. But, one, I knew Spider would hunt me down if I ratted on him, and two…I don't know…I guess I felt like I needed to take responsibility for what I'd done. *I* took the backpack to the mall. I shouldn't have, but I did. No one put a gun to my head. I never even tried to say no. So no matter what, I insisted that the coke was mine and only mine.

"When I went to my hearing, I thought my life was over. Detective Alessio was pissed that she'd failed at nailing Spider, and the evidence was undisputed. I was sure I was going to be sent straight to juvie. But luckily, because it was my first offense and Brian intervened on my behalf, I was sentenced to a year of drug counseling at a special school and a year of probation.

"It wasn't that bad. I mean, the school sucked, and I hated every second there, but at least I didn't have to go to juvie. I had school from eight to three every day, and then I could go home. Unfortunately, though, my grades at the rehab school were so bad, when I returned to public high school, I had to repeat my sophomore year."

Her grip had tightened as he spoke, and he raised her fingers to his lips and kissed them, lingering over her hand for a long moment.

"How was that?"

"What?" he asked.

"Going back to the public school."

He winced. "Everyone knew I'd been busted for drugs and 'sent away' for a year. Turns out people aren't really eager to be friends with an ex-con."

"You're not an—"

"Hannah," he said, giving her a look, "I sort of am."

She didn't fight him. "Keep going."

"But I was tall and in good shape. They had a

decent weight room at the rehab school. Anyway, that's when I met Coach Gardiner. Coach G. Swim team coach at Medford High. He changed my life. He didn't see me as a bad influence, just a kid who'd lost his way temporarily. He gave me a spot on the team."

"That's because you're *not* a bad influence," she whispered. "You just made a mistake. You're a good person, Liam Callahan."

His breath caught, and his eyes still burned as he stared back at her. She was all sweetness and understanding, and damn it, he didn't deserve her, but he couldn't bear sitting beside her anymore without holding her. He tugged her toward him. "Come sit with me."

"Where?"

Releasing her hand, he patted the lounger cushion.

Her eyes widened. "Like, sh-share your chair?"

"Yeah."

"I don't think we can both…fit," she whispered, wincing at the last word.

He huffed softly. "Okay, Hannah. We're going to do this right now. Are you listening?"

She nodded, her eyes wide and her lips parted as she stared at him with a mixture of hope and fear.

"You are *beautiful*, Hannah Giacomina. You hear me saying that? You're curvy, yeah, but I *like* that. I can't even think of the words to tell you how much I like the way you look. You've taken a few shots at yourself tonight, and I need you not to do that anymore. Not in front of me, anyway, because here's what I know: you're so beautiful, I feel it *here* every time I look at you." He placed his palm flat over his heart and tapped twice like a heartbeat. "So get up off your gorgeous, curvy ass and come sit with me. I promise you, we'll fit."

Hannah

Hannah's eyes had already been glassy from listening to the emotional story of how Liam had acted out during some dark times in his life, but his simple declaration and command reached into her chest and squeezed her heart.

You're so beautiful, I feel it here *every time I look at you.*

As she untucked her feet and stood up on shaky

legs, a huge lump rose up in her throat. She felt helpless and uncertain, but Liam didn't let her overthink it. He scooched back on the lounger, lying on his side and looking up at her. Then he patted the cushion again.

Hannah took a deep breath and eased next to him, lying on her side and facing him. He smiled at her, reaching his arm across her waist and pulling her a little closer. She pillowed her head on her bent elbow and stared at his face, now only a few millimeters from hers.

Impulsively, she leaned forward and pressed her lips to his, inhaling his scent of soap and firewood. His fingers curled into her sweater as they kissed, their breath mingling, their hearts racing.

"Hannah," he groaned, leaning away to look into her eyes. "Any q-questions? About me? About what h-happened?"

"No," she said softly, staring at his handsome face in the mix of firelight and moonlight and wishing tonight never had to end.

"*I* have one," he murmured. "Now, will you go out with me?"

She smiled at him and nodded. "Which play?"

"I'll be home in two weeks to get ready for

school. Whatever play you want."

"*Romeo and Juliet*'s playing through September," she said.

"Perfect," he murmured, leaning forward to kiss her again. When he drew back, he raised one eyebrow. "So that's a yes?"

She nodded. "That's a yes."

"Really?"

"Really."

His chest heaved into hers as his lips found hers again, demanding and hungry. Hannah whimpered softly, reaching up to lock her hands around his neck.

When she finally drew back, her lips felt raw and rosy, and her breath was broken and shallow. What was happening to her? What was happening between them? Could she even stop it now if she wanted to? Because she *didn't* want to, but it frightened her to let someone in when she'd done such a good job of keeping herself safe all these years.

"Hannah?" he asked. "What just happened here? What's going on in that head?"

"I...I just..." She unlooped her arms from his neck, resting one under her head and the other between their chests like a broken wing.

"What? Tell me. I just told you the worst of my

past, and you…you made me feel like it was okay. You can tell me anything."

She took a deep breath and swallowed, holding his eyes. "This scares me a little bit."

He shifted slightly away from her, though he kept his arm draped over her waist. "What? *This?* You and me hanging out?"

"It feels like *more* than just hanging out," she said slowly, wondering if he felt the same.

She was relieved when he nodded and said, "Yeah, it does."

"Why does it feel like that?"

His lips turned up as he answered her. "I don't know. Things like this happen in the movies: two people meet by chance and just"—he snapped his fingers—"click."

"This isn't a movie."

He shrugged. "Something about you makes sense to me."

She nodded, her own small smile an answer to his. "Something about you makes sense to me too."

"It's kind of…" He chuckled softly, shrugging again. "I don't know. Cool. Exciting. I like talking to you. I like making you laugh. I'd rather be here spending time with you than anywhere else in the world. I like you, Hannah—*really* like you—just the way you are."

Oh, my heart.

They were the exact words she'd always wanted to hear from a boy, and she beamed at him, amazed that telling him about her worries had essentially eliminated them.

"When I went to Bree's wedding today, I just thought I'd sit in a chair all alone in the back row and watch her get married. Maybe drink a glass of champagne by myself and then slip out as soon as I could. I didn't bank on you."

"Me neither. But I wouldn't change a second." He dipped his head and kissed her on the tip of her nose.

It had to be getting close to eleven now, and her eyes were feeling heavy. "Do you have to go? Can you stay?"

He pulled his arm from her waist and took his phone out of his pocket. "Let me text my dad." He typed a quick message and a moment later, his phone dinged. "He said it was okay and to be safe."

Hannah yawned. "Sorry. So tired."

He leaned forward to kiss her, then said, "Flip over."

She flipped to her other side, with her back to his front and his arm still around her. He pulled her into the spoon of his body, and Hannah could feel his warm breath on the back of her neck. The fire snapped and crackled, and the cicadas sang their songs, and she decided that nothing—not anything in her whole life—had ever felt as wonderful as this.

"I head home this Friday, the twenty-fourth. The following Friday kicks off the Labor Day festival weekend at OSF," Liam whispered. "Are you free? For the play?"

She nodded. "Mm-hm."

Just as she was drifting off, she heard his voice again, soft and tentative near her ear. "Hey, Hannah. Are you still awake?"

"Barely," she murmured.

"What made you change your mind?" he asked.

"You, Liam." She sighed, drifting off to sleep. "*You* did."

Chapter Six

Hannah

Waking up hours later to a cold fire and colder air, they were too tired to do anything but make their way to Bree's living room couch, where they quickly fell back to sleep spooned together.

When Hannah woke up the next morning, it took her a minute to figure out where she was, and with whom, until her memories of the previous night rushed back to her and she turned in Liam's arms to look at his sleeping face.

Tenderness overwhelmed her as she looked at his features. His long black lashes fanned the crescent under his eyes, and black stubble shadowed his strong jaw. His buzz cut of short black hair, which had probably been shaved off for his last swim meet, came to a rounded peak over the center of his forehead, and she remembered how those hairs at the back of his neck felt under her fingers—surprisingly soft, not bristly.

She dropped her eyes to his lips, which were pink and still a little chapped, and she made a mental note to swipe some ChapStick on them sometime soon. Then she blushed, thinking she didn't have a right to take care of him like that, though she liked it that she wanted to. She wanted to take care of him. She'd known him for such a short amount of time; it wasn't like he was her boyfriend or anything. Heck, they wouldn't even technically be dating until he picked her up on Friday. But they both seemed to realize that this wasn't some random wedding hookup. It was different. It was special.

"Date, wife, Mina, Hannah…you going to stare at me all morning or kiss me hello?" His voice was raspy and deep from sleep as one eye peeked open.

"I haven't brushed my teeth yet," she said, feeling shy.

"Then kiss me here," he said, pointing to a spot high on his cheek just under his eyes.

Hannah leaned up and placed her lips where he told her to, then leaned back to smile at him.

"And here," he whispered, closing his eyes and

pointing to his eyelid.

She dropped her lips again, as softly as she could, to the delicate skin.

"And here too," he said, pointing to the very edge of his lips.

She grinned, leaning forward to kiss him again, but as her lips touched his skin, he shifted just enough so that her lips fell flush on his.

She gasped in surprise and he grinned at her. "How can you possibly look this beautiful first thing in the morning?" he asked.

She blushed, shaking her head. "I don't know what to say when you tell me things like that."

"You should always tell the truth," he said, rubbing his thumb gently over her lower lip. "You should say 'Liam, I look this beautiful because I'm looking at you.'"

A wave of something fluttery and breathtaking crashed over her body, making her toes curl as she stared into his blue eyes, which were lightly crinkled at the edges from smiling at her.

"Liam," she said softly, "I look this beautiful because I'm looking at you."

His smile disappeared, his eyes darkening as he kissed her again. His body moved instinctually against hers, pressing closer.

"I didn't expect you to actually say it."

She smiled, flattening her hands on his chest. "You said to tell the truth."

"Then here's some more truth," he said. "When we say good-bye today, I'm not going to be able to concentrate on anything but seeing you again."

She gulped, staring up at him, not sure of what to say. He was like a runaway train, and though she wanted to jump on board and race to the end of the tracks with him, the sensible part of her insisted that they were still new to one another.

"Too much?" he asked.

She winced, not wanting to hurt him. "A little?"

"Too fast?"

She nodded. "A little."

"Too much and too fast," he confirmed, coloring a little and laughing ruefully. He rolled away from her, hitting the floor on his knees, then stood up, stretching and yawning.

As Hannah lay on her back watching him, confusion made her eyes well up with unexpected tears. Losing the warmth of his body beside hers felt sad. Thinking about two weeks apart made her feel sad too.

"Mind if I wash up a little?" he asked.

She gestured to the back hallway. "First door on your left."

"Got it."

He turned to leave the room, and she felt a tear roll out of her eye as she listened to his feet get softer and softer.

She swung her own feet to the floor, pulling down the edge of her sweater, which had ridden up while they slept. What was going on with her? Her feelings were all over the place—scared, excited, tender. Blissfully happy to wake up beside him. Nervous to move too fast. Sad that she'd pushed him away and embarrassed him. Worried that he'd decide she wasn't worth the effort.

She had no idea what would end up happening between her and Liam, but seeing him again and continuing whatever they'd started this weekend was something she wanted. *Really* wanted. On some level, in some small way, it felt like he belonged to her. And she wanted to belong to him too.

She took a deep breath and twisted her neck to look at the clock over the TV. Ten-oh-five. She stood up, stretching as he had, thinking about how his long body looked as he'd reached his arms almost to the ceiling. There was no one as beautiful as he was, and he was into *her*. She grinned to herself, spinning in a circle and catching a look at the clock again. Ten-oh-six. Ten-oh-six. What a beautiful time of—

Wait! What?!

Ten-oh-six?! Oh, no! The bridal brunch is starting in twenty-four minutes!

She sped down the hallway, knocking on the bathroom door. "Liam? We have to be back the vineyard in—"

He'd opened the door as she spoke, and the breath was knocked out of her lungs as she stared at him, shirtless and glistening, in her sister's bathroom doorway.

Liam

Liam couldn't hear what she was saying through the door, but it certainly sounded important to her, so without thinking, he'd opened the door to hear her better.

As he watched her lips open and her eyes widen,

he realized that his chest was completely bare. He hadn't wanted to get his shirt all wet as he washed his face, so he'd hung it on the back of the bathroom door.

"I...I, um...I..." She wetted her lips and finally dragged her eyes up his chest to his face, looking slightly dazed. "There's a—a brunch...thing."

He grinned at her, changing his position just slightly to cross his arms, which made his pecs and biceps bulge that much more. A small noise escaped from her throat, and he tried not to laugh.

"Hannah?"

"Hmm?" she asked, staring at the place where his muscular arms crossed.

"Hannah?"

Still frozen in place, she answered with a breathy "Yeah?"

"Eyes up."

Her cheeks flushed bright red as her eyes cut to his.

He couldn't help it. He laughed as he watched the heat seep into her face, loving how much he affected her. He'd felt a little deflated when she'd suggested he was being too eager, so it felt good to see her lose it a little while she stared at his body.

She cleared her throat. "There's a brunch in…twenty minutes. Can you, um, be ready to go in twenty minutes?"

"Sure," he shrugged, knowing exactly what his muscles looked like as he made the small gesture. "Can *you*?"

"Yes," she said quickly, pressing her palms to her cheeks, then turning quickly to head down the hallway in the other direction.

He watched with unconcealed admiration, making certain she caught him ogling as she turned at Bree's bedroom door to take one last look at him. He beamed at her, waggling his fingers. She huffed, pushing the bedroom door open and closing it again with a slam.

And he couldn't help but wonder if the Friday after next suddenly felt a little far away to Hannah too.

Hannah

Thirty minutes later, Liam and Hannah walked into

the breakfast room of the I Tri Merli hand in hand. In the car ride over to the brunch, Hannah had looked over at Liam, who looked beyond cute with his stubbled jaw and freshly ironed white shirt, courtesy of Bree's well-equipped laundry room.

"Okay," she said. "Next weekend."

He glanced at her, his expression impassive. "What happens next weekend?"

"You come over to my apartment."

He did a double take, but his face split into a grin as he caught on to her meaning. "Oh, I do?"

"Mm-hm," she said, turning toward him and crossing her legs. She'd changed into a denim skirt with a simple black camisole and black cardigan sweater, and she noticed that he kept checking out her legs, which she loved.

"And what do I do there?"

"You have dinner with me and my mom."

"We're going to have dinner with your mom?"

"Mm-hm."

"And then?" he asked.

"We can go to a movie."

"Dinner and a movie, huh? What time?"

"Six?"

He nodded. "Sounds good."

A thrill shot through her as he agreed to a date a week earlier.

He reached for her hand, lacing his fingers through hers as they turned into the vineyard parking lot. "What made you change your mind?"

"You were right. Thirteen days is too far away."

"Do we have time for me to kiss you before going in?"

She grinned back at him. "Just enough."

Hannah squeezed his hand tighter as they walked into the breakfast room. The rush of touching him, the pride she felt standing beside him as they walked inside together made her chest swell with feeling.

Is this what love feels like? she wondered. *Like you're the luckiest girl in the world because his fingers are tangled together with yours?*

Bree's eyes flitted to their locked hands, and Hannah's cheeks flushed, but she kept herself from rolling her eyes as Bree beamed at her.

"Having fun?" she asked her little sister.

"The best time ever," confirmed Hannah.

Liam

Liam pulled out one of two empty seats for Hannah to sit beside her sister and then sat down next to her, with Abby on his other side.

"You haven't forgotten, have you?" Abby raised an eyebrow at Liam. "We've got that tour bus coming in"—she looked at her watch—"ten minutes. The ladies' group from Sacramento. Remember? You told me you'd handle the tour?"

Damn it. He *hadn't* remembered that he had to work today. He wasn't thinking about anything except how much more time he had left with Hannah, and now that time was just about over. The tour he was giving would go on for an hour, and coupled with the complimentary wine tasting, he'd be tied up until one. Hannah already told him she was heading back to Oregon directly after the wedding brunch. Her packed bag was in his car, and her car was here at the vineyard, where she'd left it last night.

"Sure," he said. "I'll just have a cup of coffee and then head over, okay?"

"Of course," said Abby, turning back to her conversation with Scott.

Liam turned to Hannah, who looked up at him

with questions in her eyes.

"I promised Abby I'd help out today so she wouldn't need to leave the brunch. Sorry, I totally forgot."

"That's okay."

"At least we have Saturday on the calendar," he said. "I'll leave Medford at four and get to you around six."

"Okay," she said. "And I'll drive to you the following weekend for the play."

"Can you stay over at my mom's?"

She grimaced. "I doubt my mom will go for that, but I can ask."

He nodded, knowing it was a long shot. He leaned closer to her. "How can I get another kiss before you go?"

"I'll walk you over to the tasting room?"

He nodded, took a big gulp of his coffee, and turned to Abby. "Well, I guess I'll head over."

Hannah popped up beside him. "I'll just walk Liam over, Bree. I'll be right back."

Bree winked at her sister. "Take your time, Hannah."

Liam clasped her hand in his and led her out of the room, his heart racing as he realized that this was the last moment he'd have with her until next weekend. He pulled her down an access hallway and backed her up against the wall as his hands fell to her hips.

His lips landed urgently on hers, remembering, branding, imprinting, making her breathless and pliant in his arms as his hands slipped around to her back. She moaned, and he swallowed it, his tongue sliding against hers as she arched into him, the back of her head anchoring her to the wall behind.

"Saturday," he half murmured, half growled.

"Saturday," she repeated, resting her forehead against his. "I'll, um, text you my address."

"Yeah, good. That's, um, only six days."

"Don't count today," she said, her breath coming in short pants against the exposed skin of his open shirt. "Or Saturday. Then it's only five."

"Five days. Yeah, okay."

"Five days," she whispered.

She reached up, holding his cheeks in her hands, and pulled his face down to hers, tilting her head so that their lips fit perfectly together, and she kissed him tenderly—with hunger, but with care—and his heart shattered and rebuilt itself in her image, beating only for her.

I'm coming back here to marry her someday, he thought to himself, pulling her as close to him as he could. She was like a miracle to him, and he was sure he'd never get enough of her—the way she kissed, the way she laughed, the sweet music of her voice.

"I have to go back," she said, kissing him once more.

"I know," he said, dropping his forehead to hers again. "This was the best wedding ever."

She chuckled softly, and it made him smile.

"I agree. The *best*."

He loosened his hands from her back, sliding them from around her waist and finally letting her go.

"Saturday," she said again. "See you then."

He nodded, and she slipped away from the wall, heading back down the hallway without looking back. He clenched his jaw and took a deep breath, trying not to feel sad. He'd somehow managed to meet the girl of his dreams, and she'd somehow ended up liking him just as much as he liked her.

And like she said, if he didn't count today or Saturday, he'd see her in five short days.

Chapter Seven

Hannah

Hannah smoothed her hair, walking back toward the breakfast room, but she must have taken a wrong turn in the labyrinth-like corridors of the winery, because she ended up near the main entrance. Remembering that the breakfast room had windows overlooking the vast rows of grapes, she followed a sign with an arrow toward the vineyard.

Her heart was so full, she felt like she was walking on air, and she could barely wait to get home, because she'd be that much closer to seeing Liam again. She couldn't wait to introduce him to her mom. "This is Liam," she would say, and her mother would know—from the tone of her voice and the way her eyes shined—that the *whole* story was this: "This is

Liam…and he belongs to *me*."

And that was when she realized it: Hannah Giacomina believed in love. She believed it was *possible*, as it had been for her mother and father. For Bree and Todd. And maybe—just maybe, someday—for her and Liam.

She smiled to herself, lacing her hands behind her back and twirling in a happy circle as she walked slowly toward the pond, considering a quick detour to the tasting room so she could throw her arms back around his neck and—

Familiar voices stopped her in her tracks.

"He's *trouble*, Bree. That's why."

"He's not. He's a good kid. He's cleaned up his life, Todd."

"You don't know. I'm friends with his dad. He dealt drugs."

Bree sighed. "He told me all about what happened. It was a mistake, Todd. Not to mention, I've worked with him all summer. I've gotten to know him. I trust him."

Hannah leaned against the wall around the corner from where her sister and Todd were arguing. She knew she should make her presence known, but once she realized they were talking about her and Liam, she couldn't help but listen.

"You shouldn't, Bree. Not with your little sister."

"Come on, Todd. Don't you believe someone that young can change? He's straightened out. He's on a swim team, he worked hard here all summer—"

"You're always so eager to see the good in everyone, Bree. I love you for it, but Hannah seems so innocent. Don't you feel like you should protect her?"

"From Liam Callahan? No. Anyway, we don't know how serious it is. For heaven's sake, he was just doing me a favor by looking after her to earn a little extra spending money. It's probably nothing. A little flirtation they'll both forget about by tomorrow."

Wait. What? A favor? For...for spending money?

"I hope to God you're right about him."

"I am, Todd. Now come on. Let's get back to the brunch, okay?"

The air leaked out of Hannah's lungs until they burned as painfully as her eyes. He was doing Bree a *favor*? Bree had *asked* Liam to be her date and *paid* him for it?

You know, I think we're the only two people here tonight under thirty. Want to be my wedding date, Hannah Giacomina?

She curled her fingers into her hands, fisting them until they hurt.

Stupid, stupid, stupid Hannah!

Of course. Why else would someone as beautiful as Liam be interested in someone as fat and boring as her?

It had all been an act. A favor to Bree. A way to earn a little spending money.

Oh, my God, Hannah…could you possibly *be more stupid?*

All of her insecurities and fears rose to the surface, insisting that she should have protected herself better and berating her as a fool for ever believing that his sweet words were anything more than a favor to her sister.

Hannah's heart twisted painfully, and suddenly she couldn't catch her breath. She pressed her palm to her chest, remembering how that palm had held his face just a few minutes ago as she stupidly kissed him, believing that he belonged to her, that love could be real. What a foolish girl. He'd just been showing her a good time as a favor to her sister.

"I have to go," she murmured aloud, swiping at her cheeks, unable to keep the tears from falling just as Bree came walking around the corner.

"Hannah?" She took one look at Hannah's broken face and gasped. "Oh, no! Oh, Hannah. You heard all of that? No, it's not like we said. He seems to really—"

"You paid him?"

"It's not like that."

"It's *exactly* like that! Your fat, awkward sister can't get a date, so you *paid* someone to be my date."

"Hannah, no!" said Bree, opening her arms and trying to pull her sister into an embrace.

Hannah sobbed, fending off Bree's hugs and racing to the car. She wanted the earth to swallow her up so she wouldn't have to deal with the pain and humiliation of ever seeing Liam Callahan again. If that wasn't an option, she just wanted to get in her car and get as far away from I Tri Merli as possible. She gasped twice, trying to hold back the tears that threatened to fall in torrents.

"Wait! Hannah!" Bree ran after her. "Talk to me. Please!"

"I'm going home," she sobbed, opening her car door and sliding inside.

As she pulled out of the I Tri Merli parking lot, she didn't look back, her jagged sobs keeping her company all the way home.

Liam

Liam finished the final tasting and waved good-bye to the twelve old ladies as they climbed back aboard their "party bus," headed to another vineyard. As he turned around to walk back into the tasting room, he found Bree and Abby standing there, stricken expressions on their faces.

"What happened?" he asked. "Is everything okay?"

Bree clutched her hands together nervously, looking like she was about to throw up. It made a chill shoot through him.

"What's going on?"

"Um," said Abby, "let's sit down for a second, huh?"

And then he knew as it hit him like a sucker punch to the gut: it had to do with Hannah.

"Where's Hannah?"

"Sh-she left," said Bree. "Come sit down. I need to talk to you."

Leading the way to her office, Bree closed the door once all three of them were inside. She turned to him, still wringing her hands.

"I think I really may have messed this up for you," she said quietly.

"Messed up what?" he asked, fear and worry battling for precedence in his head and making his voice low and taut.

"Hannah."

Bree and Abby sat down at a small conference table, but Liam didn't want to sit down. He backed up to lean against the door instead.

Bree took a deep breath. "Todd and I were arguing outside...um, between the tasting room and the event space. He was saying that I shouldn't have trusted you with my sister. And I...I answered that you were just doing me a favor by looking after Hannah. That I was planning to...pay you."

It's true that's how things had started, but they'd changed almost as soon as Liam met Bree's sister. He'd fallen for her almost at first sight.

"It turned into more than that," he said.

"I can see that."

"You didn't pay me."

"Not yet."

"I don't need any money."

"I know," said Bree.

"So…what's the problem?" asked Liam, relaxing just a little. "Are you worried I won't treat her right? Because I will. And I told her all about my past, Bree. I'm not keeping secrets from her. I think she's amazing. I wouldn't do anything to mess this up."

"I know that. I—" Tears filled Bree's eyes as her face fell. "Liam, she—she overheard us. Hannah. She overheard everything we said. About you being trouble, and how you were only hanging out with her as a favor to me. She heard me say that I was planning to pay you. She heard everything."

"Oh, my God," he gasped.

"I'm so, so sorry, Liam. She—she got into her car and left right away. I've never seen anyone so crushed in my entire life."

"Oh, my God," said Liam again, covering his face with his hands before running them over his hair and clasping them on top of his bristly head. "She thinks I was just doing you a favor? She thinks I was paid to hang out with her?"

Bree nodded. "I'm so sorry."

Inside, his heart kicked up to dangerous levels of hammering. Inside, he was sweating and worried and furious. Inside, he was cutting to the chase and weighing the possibility of the most untrusting girl he'd ever known ever trusting him again. He lived his life thankful for the grace of second chances, but this looked bad. *Really* bad.

"Then what?" he asked, leaning his head back against the door.

"She left," Bree repeated in a whisper. "She was crying, and then she ran to her car and left."

"And you let her go," he said in a quiet, accusatory tone.

"I'm *so* sorry," Bree said again, wiping away a tear that slid down her cheek.

Abby tilted her head to the side, her face worried. "Liam, surely you can explain to her that it started out as a favor to Bree but that you genuinely grew to like her and—"

"You don't know her like I do, Abby. You don't know how mistrusting she is. You don't know how hard it was to get past those barriers."

"God, Liam, I am so—"

He held up his hand, trying to maintain control over his voice when he felt like screaming. "Stop, Bree. I know you're sorry. I know you didn't mean to hurt her, or me, but damn it, I don't know how to fix this, and I really—damn it, I really, *really* like her."

He pulled out a chair and sat down at the table, his mind a wreck. In the space of two hours, he'd gone from the euphoria of having Hannah in his life and falling head over heels for her to having her gone, with the possibility that he'd never be able to get her back. He winced. Even thinking those cold, bleak words was enough to make his fingers fist on the table. He couldn't lose her. He couldn't.

There had to be a way to let her know that she wasn't just some favor he was doing for Bree—sure, it might have started out that way, but in the short amount of time they'd shared together, he'd genuinely and completely fallen for her.

He took his phone out of his back pocket. He'd write her a text. He'd tell her that it had started as a favor, but—

No, that sounded terrible. She'd never believe him.

Okay. He'd go to her mom's apartment on his way home next weekend, except—he looked down at his phone. She was supposed to text him her address, but she hadn't yet, and he knew she wouldn't now.

"Do you have her address, Bree?"

Bree nodded, but even as Liam walked through

that plan, he had a feeling she wouldn't see him even if he showed up at her apartment. No, she'd be way too wary, too angry and confused.

Damn it. DAMN IT. He just needed one chance to let her know—one chance to tell her how he felt, and he was pretty sure that's all he'd get: one chance. He couldn't mess it up. He needed to figure out a way to captivate her so that she'd be too *blown* away to *look* away.

He forced his mind to go back through their hours and hours of conversation while Bree and Abby sat silently at the table.

Meeting, discussing their future plans, their parents' mistakes, Shakespeare, a soliloquy, a kiss under a weeping willow, nicknames, a dance, Shakespeare, a fire, more kissing, Shakespeare, Shakespeare, Shakespeare. He heard his own voice in his head saying, *I might even be able to take you backstage. I'm sure Julia would give us a tour of the Allen Elizabethan Theatre.*

A plan came alive in his mind, and he closed his eyes for a second in relief. No, it might not work, but it was his *best* chance.

He looked up with grim eyes. "Bree, you owe me, right?"

"Yes. A hundred percent." Bree nodded eagerly. "I'll do *anything* to make this right."

"Okay. Listen. Get her to the Allen Elizabethan Theater next Saturday night for the eight o'clock show of *Romeo and Juliet*. I don't care what you have to do. Just make sure she's there. No matter what."

Hannah

Hannah's mother had always offered a ready shoulder for crying, and Hannah had told her everything about the weekend. How she met a boy. How she fell hard for him and thought he had for her. How it turned out he'd only been doing a favor for her half-sister.

Wendy looked helplessly and sympathetically at her daughter, asking if it was possible that Liam had started their acquaintance as a favor to Bree but ended it falling for Hannah. As much as Hannah wanted to believe that was possible, she couldn't afford to open herself up to that sort of hope when it would probably just cause her more pain.

When she headed to bed that night, her spirits

were low, and she was beyond exhausted. But worst of all, she was missing Liam. She didn't know how it was possible to care for someone so intensely, so fiercely after such a short acquaintance and such a painful betrayal, but she did. She just wished she didn't.

The truth was that something had already been irreversibly changed in Hannah.

She knew what it felt like to fall for someone— the rush, the excitement, the certainty. The way his lips caressed her skin, the hum of his voice in her ear, the teasing way he smiled at her. Even if it hadn't been real to him, it was real to her, and it had opened a window into how love could be, how love could feel. She believed in love now. And now that she knew it, she couldn't deny its existence. All she could do was hope it died quickly and released her from its merciless hold.

Finally she couldn't bear it anymore, and she grabbed her phone off the bedside table in the dark and sat up, saying a quick prayer before looking for a text message from Liam. Seeing none, her eyes welled again. As she lay back down, she remembered how her day had started.

"Liam," she said in a shattered whisper, "I look

this beautiful because I'm looking at you."

And then she turned over, buried her face in her pillow, and cried herself to sleep.

Chapter Eight

Hannah

Monday was hell.

Hannah woke up with puffy eyes, opting to stay in bed all day and read *Romeo and Juliet*, occasionally checking her phone for messages from Liam, and then berating herself when there were none.

There were moments when she imagined Liam texting with his swimmer friends, telling them about this ridiculous fat girl who'd glommed onto him all weekend at her sister's wedding. She was hurt and disappointed in herself, disgusted that she'd been so easily played. She kept up a steady stream of internal dialogue, berating herself for letting her guard down and promising herself that she'd never be so stupid again.

But there were other moments when her mother's

words circled in her head and she'd feel hope. *Was it possible that Liam had started their acquaintance as a favor to Bree but ended it falling for me? Couldn't it be possible? Oh, please, please, couldn't it be possible?*

It didn't make any sense that he would put that much effort into getting her to go out with him, into making her feel beautiful, if he was just doing a favor for Bree. It had seemed so genuine—the way he looked at her, touched her, kissed her. A favor would have been making polite conversation and asking her to dance once or twice. What they'd shared had been special, magical—but mostly, what they'd shared had felt *real.*

A few minutes after self-hate and useless hope had been played out, Hannah would feel angry. Angry with Bree and Todd for ruining everything, with Liam for doing a favor for Bree, with herself for falling for him, and then with herself again for running away from I Tri Merli without talking to him and giving him a chance to explain.

And not that she'd pick up if he did, but *why* hadn't he called her yet to explain? Even if she wasn't ready to talk to him, she longed to hear his voice. And then she'd remember it had been her responsibility to text him her address, to reconfirm Saturday night, and since she hadn't texted to reconfirm, he probably assumed she hated him.

If he was even still interested.

If he was *ever* actually interested.

The worst of it, though, wasn't her embarrassment or hope or sadness or anger.

The worst thing of all was that her feelings for Liam were clarifying and solidifying every moment she spent away from him. Whatever uncertainty she'd felt on Sunday morning was long gone, because there's no way she would be this upset about someone who was just a passing infatuation. Her feelings for him were strong, and they were rooting within her rather than withering away. It was as though her heart refused to let go of him, refused to believe that he'd deceived her or toyed with her. The notion of losing him was unbearable, and even though she hadn't heard from him yet, her stupid, hopeful heart insisted that eventually she would, which is why she ended up crying herself to sleep again on Monday, Tuesday, Wednesday, Thursday, and Friday nights.

By Friday, she had to face the truth: no phone calls and no texts had to mean that they were over.

And her bruised heart felt utterly shattered.

When Bree called bright and early on Saturday morning to say she was home from her honeymoon in Mexico and was coming up to Brookings to check on Hannah and take her out for dinner, Hannah tried to say no.

"Forget it," said Bree. "I won't take no for an answer. In fact, we're blowing off Brookings. I'm taking you out to dinner in Ashland, and I've already bought third-row tickets for the eight o'clock show of *Romeo and Juliet*. Aaaand I booked us a kickass hotel room so we don't have to drive back to Brookings after the show. You *have* to come with me."

"I don't think so, Bree. I just—"

"I'll pick you up at four. We'll be in Ashland by six for dinner."

"Bree, I'm just not up for—"

"Looking forward to it! See you later!"

Bree had hung up, and even though Hannah tried to call her back several more times throughout the day to cancel, Bree never picked up the phone. As the day wore on, Hannah's heart twisted with sadness, missing Liam with a searing intensity, and finally she decided that if she wasn't going to be with *him* tonight as planned, she may as well spend the evening with her sister. So regardless of her broken heart, she was ready to go at four o'clock when Bree arrived.

"Hey, Hannah. You look great," said Bree, checking out Hannah's black T-shirt and jeans as she pulled her sister into her arms.

Hannah let herself be hugged but didn't hug Bree back. She was dressed for a funeral on purpose, and she was still angry about Bree's part in all of this.

When Bree drew back, she cocked her head to the side. "Mad at me?"

Hannah nodded.

"Want to talk about it? We've got a two-hour car ride ahead, sis. I'm a good listener and I'm an even better advice-giver. I promise."

Hannah had essentially locked herself in her room all week, and even though her well-intentioned mother had stopped in to check on her and ask if she was okay a couple of times a day, she couldn't bear talking about Liam, so she'd asked to be left alone. She didn't think it would help to talk about it, but she felt so sad, she was ready to try just about anything. And who better than Bree, who knew her and knew Liam and had seen them together?

"Okay."

And thank God they had such a long car ride,

followed by an hour-long dinner near the theater, because Hannah rehashed the entirety—*every little detail*—of her weekend with Liam for her older sister.

When she got to the part about kissing under the weeping willow, Bree sighed.

Halfway to Ashland, Bree giggled over the fortysomething guest who'd forced Hannah and Liam into the charade of marriage.

As they looked for street parking halfway between the theater and the restaurant, Bree cooed as Hannah recounted their romantic dance to "In My Life."

Hannah took a big bite of her croque monsieur before telling her sister how she'd listened to the story of his arrest by the outdoor fire and had somehow ended up spooned by his side.

And Bree was so transfixed by Hannah's recounting of them waking up on the couch together that she barely had a spoonful of the chocolate mousse they were sharing before Hannah finished it.

"The way he looked at me, Bree? The way he looked at me after kissing me in that little hallway on Sunday morning? It was like a promise. It was like he was promising me something in his head. Something deep and wonderful and—and then I walked away from him and overheard you and Todd."

"And decided that he was only doing a favor for me by being nice to you."

"A *paid* favor."

"You need to know something," said Bree. "I never paid him."

"What?"

"He refused to take my money."

"He did?"

"Wouldn't take a dime. His feelings for you were real, Hannah."

"Then why hasn't he called? Or texted?"

Hannah stirred her coffee, glancing at her watch. It was only seven-thirty. They still had half an hour before the show, and the theater was only five minutes away.

"Tell me something," said Bree. "If he called you, would you pick up? Would you give him a chance to explain? Or would you jump down his throat and hang up on him?"

Hannah shrugged. "I don't know."

"How about a text? Would a text be enough? Even if it was a really great text, would it be enough?"

"I don't know," said Hannah, her voice breaking.

She couldn't imagine a text that could make this better—that could show her just how much he cared.

"Then why would he call or text? I'm sure he's as scared as you are." Bree reached across the table and took her little sister's hands in hers. "But Hannah, you know in your heart, don't you? You know that no man acts the way that Liam acted unless he's genuinely interested. No man looks at a woman the way Liam looked at you unless he's genuinely, deeply, possibly *irrevocably* interested."

Hannah took a deep breath. "That's what my heart keeps saying. And yet—"

"What?" asked Bree, releasing Hannah's hands when the check arrived.

She shrugged, feeling miserable. "It's hard to *know*. It's hard to trust him now."

Bree signed the receipt, then focused on her sister. "I know he only spent one night with you, but he got to know you pretty well. My bet is that he suspects that you won't talk to him and that reaching out might even push you further away. If he's falling for you, he's not going to risk doing anything that could hurt you more…or that could hurt his chances with you."

"He believes in second chances," said Hannah

quietly.

"Yes, he does." Bree waited a moment, scanning Hannah's face intensely. "Do *you*?"

Hannah swallowed the lump in her throat. "I don't know."

"I think you need to answer that question. Because if the answer is no, you need to forget about Liam and let him go. There's no hope for you two— for anyone, really—without second chances."

Bree stood up, and they walked out into the cool night air, strolling toward the huge theater complex only a block away.

"It still hurts sometimes that our dad cheated on my mom," said Bree, reaching for Hannah's arm as they walked side by side. "He broke her heart. And you know? I could have let my father's cheating ruin my chances at love. I could have decided that I didn't trust men. But I didn't. Falling in love with Todd was the best thing that ever happened to me. The best, Hannah. Was I afraid of getting hurt? Of course. But you can't let your fears and insecurities take control of your heart."

Hannah thought about this. About her fears that no boy could see beyond her big body and love her heart, but maybe it had actually happened. And if

Liam came to her and explained, apologized, and asked for another chance? Maybe she should give it to him.

Taking Hannah's silence as permission to continue, Bree said, "I saw you walk into that breakfast room last Sunday like you were on top of the world, holding hands with a beautiful boy who looked so proud to be standing beside you. I asked him to look after you at the wedding, yes. I offered to pay him, but he refused to take my money, Hannah. Why? Because the way you felt about each other, the way you looked at each other…that wasn't about a favor or the promise of a little spending money. That was *you*. And *him*. And…and fireworks. Don't let anyone, or anything, take that away from you."

Hannah sniffled lightly as her tired eyes pooled with tears. And something tight and angry inside of her loosened up as Bree's words lodged deeply in her heart. Synapses fired, and her chest swelled as a montage of the weekend played like a movie in her mind.

Are you here with anyone?

Want to be my wedding date, Hannah Giacomina?

If you believed in true love, we'd be a match

made in heaven.

If you were going to ask which part of her is so distracting, I'd have no choice but to show you.

I wouldn't have asked you out if I was seeing someone. I don't do that. I'm not with anyone right now, Hannah...except you.

Dance with me, wife.

Nothing's going to happen unless you want it to. I promise.

My goal by the end of tonight is for you to say yes.

You are beautiful, Hannah Giacomina. You hear me saying that?

Something about you makes sense to me.

What made you change your mind?

I think it's hard for people to give second chances...

"I believe in second chances," whispered Hannah, her feet stopping on the sidewalk as she looked at Bree. "I believe in love. When you get back, will you find him and tell him that? If he calls, I'll pick up. If he texts, I'll answer. I want a second chance."

Bree grinned at her. "I can't begin to tell you how glad I am to hear that."

Liam

Liam stood in the wings of the packed Allen Elizabethan Theater, trying to stay out of the way of the actors finishing up the fifth act of *Romeo and Juliet*. Although the costume he wore was velvet, he suspected his hands were sweating more because he was nervous than because he was hot. When he'd peeked at the audience during intermission and seen Hannah and Bree sitting together in the third row, his heart had soared.

Please let this work. Please let this work.

"Almost ready?"

Liam looked up to see his mom's friend, Julia, standing beside him.

He nodded. "Yeah. And thanks for doing this."

Julia shrugged. "Don't forget. You owe me a week of work at Christmas and two weeks over spring break."

"Concessions?" he asked hopefully.

"Ticket ripping," she answered. "Now, on to

business. After the bows, John Granger, who plays Mercutio, is going to say that the guests in seats C10 and C12 have been randomly chosen to have a private preview of our new Shakespeare-inspired show. The rest of the theater will empty out. Steve, up in the box, will give you a spotlight and overhead mic, and then…" She grinned at him, pushing her glasses up to the bridge of his nose. "It's show time!"

Liam took a deep breath and nodded. "Okay. Awesome."

"She must be pretty special."

"She is," he said. "She's amazing."

"Well, if I don't see you before you go on, best of luck."

"Thanks again, Julia."

"Anything for true love," she said over her shoulder, walking into the backstage shadows as Romeo drank a vial of poison on stage.

True love.

His heart raced.

Liam had no idea if what he felt for Hannah was love. His mom, who was pretty awesome, had asked him last night if his feelings for Hannah could be explained by a massive crush. He'd shrugged, playing it cool and telling her it was possible, but in his heart, he knew it was more than that. Since Hannah had left I Tri Merl last Sunday, he'd barely been able to eat, his mind had wandered endlessly to their time together, and he'd had trouble sleeping when he thought about never seeing her again. If that horrible feeling wasn't love, he didn't know what it was.

He rubbed his sweaty palms on his tan velvet pants, which were tucked into a pair of knee-high leather boots. He wore a cream-colored shirt with billowy sleeves that looked completely idiotic and a brown leather vest. He pulled the brown wide-brimmed hat off his head and played with its cream-colored feather for a second before smashing it back on his head.

Juliet was stabbing herself with a rusty dagger. It was almost—in Julia's words—*show time*.

For a guy like Liam, who was at home in a pool or working in a vineyard, this entire plan was *way* out of his comfort zone, and for a second he wondered if it was worth it to make such a fool of himself. But then he heard Hannah's voice in his head: *I look this beautiful because I'm looking at you.*

He had no choice. He'd either win her back or die—*of sheer ridiculousness*—trying.

"For never was there a story of more woe…than

this of Juliet and her Romeo."

The audience broke into applause, and Liam's heart rate doubled.

It's almost time. It's almost time. It's almost time.

The actors were on stage bowing, and before he knew it, he heard John Granger announcing that the theater guests in seats C10 and C12 should remain seated, as they'd been chosen for a sneak peek into the Allen Elizabethan's new Shakespeare-inspired play.

Peeking out through a one-way scrim, he watched as Hannah's lips parted in surprise. She turned to Bree, who shrugged her shoulders with a grin and sat back down. They appeared to have a quick discussion, and then Hannah sat back down too, looking up at the stage expectantly.

Rubbing his hands together, he reached for the script he'd spent all week writing. He had no idea if it was good. He suspected it wasn't. But it was all he had.

He looked through the scrim again. The theater was about 80 percent empty now, with Bree and Hannah both staring at the stage. The last few stragglers funneled through the theater doors, the houselights went down, and suddenly, a spotlight appeared on center stage.

Show time.

Stepping out from the darkness, Liam walked across the stage until he was standing in the middle of the spotlight. Unrolling the scroll in his hands, he glanced at Hannah once before reading:

"How shall I walk this earth without her?

She beneath the willow's bough.

She 'in my life' may I woo.

She for me, right then, right now."

He swallowed, looking up to find Hannah leaning forward in her seat, her eyes fixed on him, her lips parted in surprise. He gulped, clearing his throat before continuing:

"How shall I be content without her?

She, the fairest under thirty.

She on a lounge, in the dark, by a fire,

She, who seemed, for a time, to prefer me."

"Liam?"

Hannah. He heard her voice in the audience and stopped reading, looking over the scroll at her face. Her cheeks glistened with tears, and her wobbly smile was the sweetest sight he'd seen in a week. He watched as Bree leaned closer to her sister and whispered something, then she stood up, gave Liam a double thumbs-up, and hurried up the aisle to the exit.

"Want me to keep going?" he asked.

She nodded. "Please."

"Do not take her lips away.

Nor lovely face, nor heart so true.

But give me one more chance, I pray.

I promise, my Mina, I'd never betray you."

The echo of his voice through the microphone slowly faded, and he rolled up his scroll, staring at her, wishing he could quell the racing of his heart.

Suddenly the spotlight went dark, and Liam stepped forward as the houselights came up to a dim glow. He stood at the edge of the stage, feeling ridiculous, staring at her face, hoping against hope that she had another chance in her heart to give him.

With her eyes locked on his, she stood up, sidestepped down her row, then walked down the aisle to stand beside the first row.

"Liam."

"Hannah."

"I loved it," she said softly, her voice breathless. She reached up and swiped away her tears. "I can't believe you did all of this for me."

"Hannah," he said, jumping off center stage and taking off his hat as he faced her. "I'd do almost *anything*…for another chance with you."

She bit her bottom lip before asking, "You *liked* me, right? That was real? Not just a favor to Bree?"

He took a step closer to her. "*Liked* you? No, not *liked*. I *like* you—present tense. Right here. Right now. So much. Honestly, *like* doesn't even begin to cover it, Hannah."

She took a step closer to him. "I know you didn't take the money."

"I didn't even consider it," he answered, taking another step toward her.

She exhaled shakily, a relieved smile brightening her face for a moment before her wide eyes became serious again. "I'm going to freak out sometimes. I'm going to be a little difficult, because even though I'm working on it, this is all new for me, and it's really hard for me to trust that it's real."

He took another step closer to her, smiling because he couldn't help it. He wanted to reach for her and pull her into his arms, but he also sensed she had more to say. "I'm okay with that, Hannah. I can be patient."

She took another small step in his direction. "And I might, you know, seem like I'm pushing you away sometimes, but inside all I want is for you to hold me so close and so tight that I feel like you'll never let me go."

His scroll hit the floor, he closed the distance between them, and his hands landed on her hips.

"I'll stick around, even when you push me away," he promised, pulling her closer.

She flattened her hands on his chest. "And I might *run* away sometimes while I'm figuring this out. But if—if you could just…just wait for me, I will *always* run back to you again."

"Hannah," he breathed, overwhelmed by his feelings for her, by her simple honesty as she told him that she wanted him in her life, even if she was scared too. "I'd wait forever if I had to."

"I didn't even know I was looking for you," she said. "But life is so lonesome without you now."

"For me too." He laced his fingers behind her back, flicking his eyes to her lips and staring at them, counting down the seconds until he could kiss them again, because Sunday morning was *way* too long ago.

"Liam, I…" Her voice faltered.

"Tell me," he said, looking into her eyes and encouraging her to finish so they could get on with laughing and loving and holding hands and kissing—

so they could get back to the good stuff and leave the awfulness of the past week behind.

She swallowed, looking down for a moment, perhaps to muster her courage before slamming her brown eyes into his. "Will *you* give *me* a second chance?"

He was sure that his smile took over his entire face, because he'd never heard sweeter words in his entire life. "Yes! As many as you need."

Her arms flew around his neck and her back bowed as she pressed her body flush against his. Liam picked her up off the ground, spinning her in a circle before leaning back to catch her eyes with his.

"You know," he said, looking around at the dark, empty theater before gazing down at her with a happy grin. "I think we're the only two people here tonight under thirty. Want to be my girlfriend, Hannah Giacomina?"

She nodded. "Absolutely."

And as she pulled his head down to hers for a kiss, Liam Callahan realized that while he was originally cast as a date for Hannah, he'd somehow ended up in the part of he wanted most of all.

Her boyfriend.

THE END

More from Callie

LOVE IS FOR EVERYONE

A Date for Hannah
Thank you for reading!

A Song for Lexi
Coming in February 2019

The Truth about Chase
Coming in August 2019

** Interested in talking more about A DATE FOR HANNAH? Turn the page for questions to consider! **

QUESTIONS TO CONSIDER

1. One of the themes of A DATE FOR HANNAH is the giving and taking of "second chances." Has there been a time in your life when you've been given a second chance? Is there someone in your life who could use one?

2. Hannah is insecure about the way she looks and even has an internal voice berating her for being "fat" and "ugly." Do you have an internal voice that says mean things to you? What are some ways that you could silence that voice or change it into a more positive message?

3. Hannah believes that no one could like her "for her," even though it's what she wants. She finally works up the courage to show Liam the "real" Hannah, and to her surprise, he really likes her. We all wear masks to hide parts of ourselves. Are there parts of you that you should share more?

4. Hannah often compares herself to Bree. Is it common for siblings to compare themselves to one another? How is it a positive thing and/or a negative thing?

5. Liam's mother reminds him that "If you want

someone's trust, share your honesty," but it's really hard to be honest sometimes, isn't it?

6. In different ways, Liam and Hannah both come from broken families: Liam's parents divorced when he was fourteen, and Hannah's father divorced his first wife to marry Hannah's mother. How did Liam and Hannah's family histories affect the choices they made or the way they felt about themselves?

7. Why does Liam take Spider's backpack to the mall? Have you ever felt pressured into making a bad choice? Can you think of another way that Liam could have handled that situation?

8. The book ends with Hannah and Liam in a relationship. Do you think they'll make it? What do they still need to work on to keep their bond strong?

More from Katy

THE SUMMERHAVEN TRIO

Fighting Irish
Smiling Irish
Loving Irish
Catching Irish

THE BLUEBERRY LANE SERIES

THE ENGLISH BROTHERS
(Blueberry Lane Books #1–7)

Breaking Up with Barrett
Falling for Fitz
Anyone but Alex
Seduced by Stratton
Wild about Weston
Kiss Me Kate
Marrying Mr. English

Ginger's Heart
Dark Sexy Knight
Don't Speak
Shear Heaven

Fragments of Ash
Coming 2018

Swan Song
Coming 2018

STAND-ALONE BOOKS

After We Break
(a stand-alone second-chance romance)

Frosted
(a romance novella for mature readers)

Unloved, a love story
(a stand-alone suspenseful romance)

About the Author

CALLIE HENRY is the YA pen name of *New York Times* and *USA Today* bestselling contemporary romance author Katy Regnery.

Katy claims authorship of the multititled *New York Times* and *USA Today* bestselling Blueberry Lane Series; the six-book, bestselling ~a modern fairytale~ series; the Summerhaven Trio; and several other stand-alone novels and novellas, including the 2018 RITA® nominated, *USA Today* bestselling contemporary romance *Unloved, a love story*.

Katy's books are available in English, French, German, Italian, Polish, Portuguese, and Turkish.

Katy lives in the relative wilds of northern Fairfield County, Connecticut, where her writing room looks out at the woods, and her husband, two young children, two dogs, and one Blue Tonkinese kitten create just enough cheerful chaos to remind her that the very best love stories begin at home.